VIRTUAL GIRLFRIEND

A LOVE REKINDLED THROUGH MEMORIES

SUJEET PANDEY

Contents

1

Diwali Dusk: The Lights of Home

Kunal Sharma, a 27-year-old fair-skinned and handsome man with short hair and a neatly trimmed beard, stepped out of the taxi as dusk fell over Mumbai, the city alight with the glow of Diwali. The evening air, balmy and scented with bursts of fireworks, immediately enveloped him. It had been nearly a year since his last visit home from Bangalore, where he was immersed in the bustling world of business consulting. The familiar chaos of the city, now dressed in festive finery, felt both overwhelming and comforting.

As he walked towards the family home, the streets of his old neighborhood were transformed. Every building and house shimmered under the festive illumination of countless lights and lanterns. Children ran around with sparklers, their laughter mingling with the shouts of vendors selling festive goods. The markets were a riot of color, with families gathering to buy sweets and decorations. Stalls lined the sidewalks, brimming with everything from glittering decorations to sweet treats, each manned by vendors whose cheerful banter added to the festive din. Here and there, groups of teenagers competed in impromptu fireworks displays, their laughter and shouts melding with the ongoing music from nearby speakers, which played a mix of classic songs and contemporary hits. Kunal took a moment to lean against the cool metal of a lamppost, taking in the scene. The sense of community was palpable, as neighbors shared sweets and exchanged greetings, reveling in the shared joy of the festival. It was a reminder of the Diwalis of his youth, where the entire community came together to celebrate the triumph of light over darkness.

From every open window and doorway, the joyful sounds of the neighborhood echoed through the cool evening air. The streets were a tapestry of glowing lanterns and twinkling fairy lights, stretching as far as the eye could see. Families, young couples, and groups of children gathered in small clusters, setting off an array of fireworks that painted the night sky with bursts of color.

Kunal's mind drifted to his life in Bangalore—a city that promised growth and offered a relentless pace that both thrilled and exhausted him. His career in business consulting, while flourishing, often felt like a double-edged sword. The thrill of closing deals and the adrenaline of challenging projects were frequently overshadowed by long hours and the constant pressure to perform. As he maneuvered through the festive streets, Kunal couldn't help but be excited about spending Diwali at home with his family. The memories of past celebrations filled his mind.

Kunal's family's 3BHK apartment in a bustling Mumbai suburb was alive with activity and warmly lit by the soft glow of diyas. Inside, the living room was transformed into a festive tableau, with intricately designed Rangoli colors brightening the floors and golden fairy lights draped along the balconies and windows. Each room bore the touch of careful decoration, marigold garlands hung around doorframes, and the aroma of incense wafted through the air, mingling with the scent of sweets being prepared in the kitchen.

Kunal paused at the entrance, leaning against the doorframe, unnoticed. He watched the familiar scene with a smile, the warmth of home thawing the coldness that had enveloped his heart. His father, Sunil, a retired engineer who had enjoyed a successful career in the construction industry, was adjusting the lights in the living room. His younger sister, Priya, currently pursuing a degree in computer science, was arguing they needed more color around the decorations. Meera, Kunal's mother and a retired school principal, was orchestrating the placement of every decoration with her usual grace and authority.

Suddenly, his mother turned and spotted him at the door. Her face lit up with joy. "Kunal!" Meera exclaimed, rushing towards him and enveloping him in a hug that smelled of roses and sandalwood. "You're finally here," she whispered, her voice thick with emotion. As she held him, Kunal felt a wave of relief wash over him, a feeling of security he hadn't felt in a long time. "Wouldn't miss Diwali at home, Ma," Kunal murmured, his voice muffled in his mother's shoulder. As he stepped further into the house, the family gathered around him, pulling him into their festive preparations with infectious enthusiasm. The house was filled with the aroma of spices and traditional dishes, each recipe handed down through generations and each dish a symbol of their familial love.

He was greeted by a dazzling display of decorations that spoke both of tradition and the personal touches unique to his family. The entryway was draped with strings of flowers and leaves, a symbol of prosperity and a welcome to the gods. The living room transformed into a vibrant tableau reflective of their regional roots combined with their cosmopolitan influence. The walls were adorned with paper lanterns, each handcrafted from colorful papers and lit from within to cast a soft, welcoming glow. These lanterns, a craft passed down through generations, were especially significant to Kunal's family, symbolizing the triumph of light over darkness.

The decorations on the floor were an elaborate design that combined traditional patterns with modern artistic touches. Using bright colored powders and flower petals, the design featured motifs of beauty and purity in culture. Surrounding the central design were smaller decorations leading up to the altar, representing the welcoming of prosperity into the home. On the balcony and windowsills, clay lamps, painted by Kunal's sister Priya, flickered gently. Each lamp was painted with vibrant patterns of swirls and dots, showcasing the family's artistic flair. Alongside the lamps, polished brass lamps inherited from Kunal's grandmother were filled with oil and wicks ready to be lit at dusk.

Outside, the façade of the house was illuminated by strings of lights, arranged to outline the shape of the house and twinkle like stars against the night sky. These lights not only brightened the home but also drew a stark contrast against the more traditional elements, reflecting the blend of old and new that characterized their family's approach to the festival. This harmonious blend of decorations was not just a feast for the eyes but a manifestation of the family's deep-rooted cultural pride and their joyous embrace of the spirit of the festival. Each element, carefully chosen and lovingly placed, told a story of heritage, continuity, and celebration, weaving together threads of the past with the vibrant tapestry of the present. One year, Priya and Kunal had decided to surprise their parents by taking over the festival decorations themselves. They spent hours crafting paper lanterns and stringing lights. Although they ended up tangling the entire set of lights, the laughter and teamwork from that day remained one of Kunal's fondest memories, a testament to the deep bond he shared with his sister.

Kunal decided to join his mother in the kitchen while Priya and their father continued with the decorations. He steps up beside her, taking over the task of shaping the sweets. "Let me handle these, Ma," he says, eager to be involved. Meera watches him for a moment, then nods appreciatively, her eyes bright with pride. As they work side by side, Kunal and his mother share a comfortable chat about the festivities, the joy evident in their voices. "These sweets look even better than last year's," Kunal comments, admiring their handiwork. Meera laughs, a sound that fills the room with warmth. "You say that every year, but I think it's just your sweet tooth talking." Their conversation flows easily, filled with updates from Kunal about his life in Bangalore—his latest projects, the vibrant city life, and the new friends he's made. Meera listens intently, her questions thoughtful and encouraging, showing genuine interest in his urban adventures.

As the doorbell rings, the festive atmosphere in the Sharma household peaks with anticipation. Kunal, already smiling, opens the door to find Amit, Riya, and Sohan standing there with wide grins and arms laden with gifts and sweets. The trio steps inside, their arrival bringing a fresh wave of energy into the home. "Kunal! It's been too long," Amit exclaims, clapping him on the back. He hands over a box of gourmet sweets, a nod to their childhood days of sharing treats. Riya steps forward, her embrace warm as she laughs, "Look at you, all successful and still the same!" She presents Kunal with a small, intricately painted lamp, a symbol of their lasting friendship. Sohan, ever the charismatic one, joins in with a hearty laugh. "You haven't changed a bit, man!" He hands Kunal a customized coffee mug, a humorous nod to their endless college night discussions over coffee. As they settle into the living room, Meera and Priya come in to greet the guests.

Meera, with her usual grace, welcomes them, her voice filled with genuine affection. "Amit, Riya, Sohan, it's so wonderful to see you all again. You're just in time for some homemade delicacies!" Priya, who has always admired Amit's architectural designs, strikes up a conversation with him. "I saw your latest project on social media; it's stunning! How do you come up with these ideas?" she asks, genuinely curious. Amit, pleased with the interest, explains his creative process, and they quickly delve into a discussion about art and design, Priya's questions thoughtful and insightful. Meanwhile, Riya, who has started her own digital marketing firm, shares tips with Meera on how to promote her community classes online. "You know, Auntie, a little social media presence could really expand your audience," Riya suggests enthusiastically. Sohan, always the entrepreneur, chats with Sunil about the nuances of running a café. "It's about creating an experience, not just selling coffee," he explains. Sunil, intrigued, shares his own experiences from his engineering projects that often required a deep understanding of client needs. The room buzzes with conversations, laughter mingling with the crackle of fireworks outside. Kunal looks around, a content smile playing on his lips as he watches his childhood friends interact with his family. The ease with which they all connect, bridging the gap between past and present, fills him with a warm sense of pride and joy. As the evening progresses, the group gathers around the dining table, which is laden with an array of festive dishes. They toast to their enduring friendship, share stories of their recent adventures, and reminisce about their mischievous escapades as children. The air is thick with nostalgia, yet vibrant with the excitement of their current lives. After dinner, they move to the terrace, where Priya has set up a small firework display. They light sparklers and watch the night sky lit by colorful bursts.

Feeling a mix of joy and subtle exhaustion from the emotions and journey of the day, Kunal excused himself, heading to his room under the pretense of needing a brief rest. Once in his room, Kunal closed the door softly behind him. His room, a well-kept sanctuary of order and calm, reflected his methodical and thoughtful nature. The walls were lined with bookshelves filled with an array of books, from thick volumes of poetry by the likes of Rumi and Tagore to modern business management guides. Each book was arranged neatly, their spines creating a colorful mosaic of his interests and intellectual pursuits. Beside the bookshelves, a glass cabinet displayed an impressive collection of basketball trophies, medals, and certificates from his school and college days. The polished trophies caught the soft light, each one a testament to his dedication and skill on the court.

He walked straight to the restroom, turning on the tap and splashing cold water on his face. The cool water was refreshing, washing away the fatigue of travel and the emotional residue of the day's reunions. He patted his face dry with a soft towel hanging nearby, feeling reinvigorated. Stepping back into his room, he switched on the ceiling fan, its gentle hum a comforting background noise. He then dimmed the lights to a soft glow, casting the room in a warm, inviting light that was perfect for introspection. Kunal then moved to his bed, the sheets crisp and cool against his skin as he lay down. He reached for his wallet, pulling out a worn photograph that he looked at every day. It was a photo, a reminder of the past that always seemed to draw him in. The photo captured Sakshi, about 22 years old, looking radiant as ever. Her eyes were a light shade of brown. Her hair was well-combed and carefully tucked behind her ears, framing her gently smiling face. She wore a purple round-neck top, which complemented her vibrant expression and added to her youthful allure. In the background, the faint outline of a building reminded Kunal about a day they had spent out in the city, one of their many adventures that were filled with laughter and simple joys. Her smile, wide and genuine, seemed to leap from the image, bringing a sense of warmth and happiness to anyone who viewed it. It was a smile that Kunal remembered all too well—the kind that could light up the dimmest of rooms and lift the heaviest of spirits.

As Kunal held the photo, his own face mirrored the happiness found in Sakshi's expression. It was more than just a photograph; it was a portal to a time of unguarded joy and a connection that still tugged at his heartstrings. The bond they shared was evident in the way his eyes lingered on her image, a mix of fondness and a trace of melancholy for times gone by. Lying back, he traced the outline of her face with his finger, a tender gesture filled with love. As he gazed at her image, the memories of their time together began to play in his mind like a favorite old movie, each scene both beautiful and full. From downstairs, he could hear his family and friends calling him to come down and continue the celebrations. But Kunal just lay in bed, his mind slowly drifting into a flashback as he looked at Sakshi's photo, her smiling face leading him back to the days that had once made up his whole world—the days that he spent with Sakshi.

ppp

2
The Journey to New Beginnings

6 Years Ago

The cool early morning air at Mumbai's railway station buzzed with the symphony of farewells and announcements. Kunal, amidst the sea of bustling passengers, felt the familiar clench of bittersweet emotions as he hugged each of his family members. His mother's eyes brimmed with tears, his father offered a handshake that was firm with unspoken pride, and Priya, his sister, held on to him a little longer, her embrace tight and lingering. "Take care of yourself, and call us as soon as you arrive," his mother instructed, her voice thick with emotion. "I will, Ma," Kunal reassured her, managing a smile, his heart caught between the excitement of the journey ahead and the ache of departure. With a final wave, he boarded the train, weaving through the corridor to find his reserved side lower berth. As the train whistled to life, marking the beginning of his new chapter, Kunal settled into his seat, his backpack stowed neatly above. The window seat he had secured was ideal, not just for the comfort but for the views it offered—a perfect canvas to witness the changing landscapes of India.

Kunal's heart raced with a mix of excitement and apprehension as the train pulled away from the platform, each chug echoing the beat of his pulse. The cityscape of Mumbai slowly receded into the background, and with it, the life he had always known. As buildings blurred into green fields, Kunal felt a twinge of longing—a string tethered to his heart, pulling him back even as he moved forward. He leaned back against the seat, closing his eyes momentarily, allowing himself to feel the full weight of his decision. He was leaving behind more than just a city; he was stepping away from the cocoon of his family, the comfort of familiar streets, and the routine that had defined his daily existence. The reality of his solitude struck him with a startling clarity. He was alone now, truly on his own for the first time.

In the quiet hum of the train's motion, Kunal's thoughts drifted to the dreams that had propelled him here—to chase a degree in business at one of the country's premier universities. He envisioned himself in lecture halls, surrounded by peers as ambitious as himself, engaging in debates that stretched into the night, and finding his place among future leaders. The excitement of these prospects filled him with a sense of purpose, and yet, the unknowns whispered doubts that clouded his mind. "What if I don't fit in? What if the challenges are greater than I anticipate?" he wondered silently. The blend of excitement and anxiety churned inside him, a storm that both motivated and daunted him.

Opening his eyes, Kunal gazed out the window again, watching the landscape shift slowly as the train ascended through varying terrains. Each kilometer traveled was a step toward his future, a physical manifestation of his metaphorical journey toward personal and professional growth. He felt a resolve building within him, a determination to embrace the opportunities and overcome the obstacles that awaited him. "This journey is mine to make," Kunal murmured to himself, a quiet assertion over the clatter of the tracks. "Every challenge is a stepping stone to my dreams." With that thought, a sense of peace settled over him, mingling with his resolve. He was ready to face the new life that awaited him, armed with the lessons of his past and the dreams of his future.

As the train chugged along, Kunal's eyes were drawn to the transformation of the landscape unfurling outside his window. The dense, skyscraper-filled skyline of the city gave way to the open, lush expanses of the countryside. As the train snaked through the Western Ghats, he was greeted by a spectacular tapestry of verdant greenery and rugged terrain. The monsoon rains had painted the valleys a deep emerald, and waterfalls cascaded down the mountainsides, creating ribbons of white foam that sparkled under the morning sun. The transition was not just visual but sensory. The clamor of the city's traffic was replaced by the rhythmic clacking of the train over the tracks, a soothing soundtrack to the scenic views. The air grew fresher, cooler, and tinged with the earthy scent of rain-soaked soil—a stark departure from the smog and salt of Mumbai. Occasionally, the train passed through tunnels, and the sudden darkness was a thrilling contrast to the bright light of day, each emergence like a rebirth into a new world.

Kunal watched as the flat landscapes started to become more undulating, turning into rolling hills and then into steeper gradients as the train approached the mountainous regions. Each bend in the tracks offered a new vista: small villages with terracotta-roofed houses, fields dotted with farmers at work, children playing by the tracks, and women laying out colorful saris to dry on the bushes. As the train climbed higher, the air grew noticeably cooler, and Kunal wrapped his shawl tighter around him. From his window, he could see the dense forests of pine and deodar trees, their needles glistening with moisture. Occasionally, a burst of wildlife—a group of monkeys scampering along a ridge, or a lone peacock strutting majestically across a clearing—added a pulse of life to the serene landscape.

As evening approached, the setting sun cast long shadows over the valleys, and the sky turned a palette of deep oranges and purples. The train chugged along, its whistle echoing through the hills, a lonely but comforting sound that seemed to announce Kunal's impending arrival into a new phase of his life. This journey, a bridge between his past and his future, was marked by a profound sense of transition—not just in the physical landscapes but also within Kunal, as he pondered the roads he had traveled and the paths that lay ahead. Kunal unpacked the food his mother had prepared—a box filled with sandwiches, parathas, and some of her special ladoos. Each bite was a reminder of home, the flavors mingling with his senses, bringing both comfort and a pang of homesickness. During the meal, Kunal struck up a conversation with an elderly woman sitting opposite him. She was traveling to visit her son and his family. As they shared snacks, the woman recounted stories of her own travels in her younger days, her voice rich with nostalgia and wisdom. Kunal listened, engaged, his natural empathy drawing him into her stories.

"Life, my dear, is a series of such journeys," she said thoughtfully, her eyes crinkling with a smile. "Each person we meet carries a lesson we're meant to learn." Kunal nodded, feeling a deep connection with her words. They resonated within him, sparking a contemplation about what lessons awaited him in Dehradun. The journey from Mumbai to Dehradun, over twenty-seven hours long, provided Kunal with ample time to reflect. As the train eased into Dehradun station, the chaos of arrival burst forth like a scene from a vibrant tapestry. The platform was a flurry of activity; porters called out in strong, melodious tones, offering to carry luggage, while families and students clamored around, each engrossed in their joyful reunions and eager departures. The air buzzed with the dialects of Hindi and Garhwali, blending into a lively symphony that welcomed Kunal to this new chapter of his life.

Stepping onto the platform, he thought to himself, "I'm on my own now, and my career journey has just started. I'm going to make it count." His thoughts were interrupted by the sharp scents of street food vendors lining the station exits. The aroma of freshly made samosas and sweet jalebis filled the air, mingling with the diesel fumes of idling cabs. Above him, the station's old colonial architecture stood in stark contrast to the modern hustle below, its weathered façade watching over the daily human drama that unfolded at its doors. Outside, the view was breathtaking. The railway station sat at the edge of the city, with the lush green hills of the lesser Himalayas in the backdrop, their peaks shrouded in a light mist. It was a scene right out of a postcard, and for a moment, Kunal was transfixed by the natural beauty and the serene calm that lay just beyond the chaotic thresholds of the station. As Kunal navigated his way through the crowd, avoiding the eager coolies and taxi drivers vying for his attention, he felt a surge of independence. Here, in this bustling station, amidst the blend of the old world charm and the frenetic pace of modern life, Kunal was just another traveler, anonymous yet part of a larger narrative. Each step he took was a further plunge into his new life, a life that promised the pursuit of knowledge and the forging of new friendships.

Pulling his luggage behind him, Kunal made his way to the taxi stand, ready to leave behind the clamor of the railway station for the quieter, studious avenues of UPES. As he settled into the back seat of the cab, the city began to unfold before him, each street corner turning a new page in his journey. The taxi wove through the busy streets of Dehradun, bustling with the daily rhythm of shopkeepers opening their stalls and locals negotiating their morning purchases. The air was cooler here, filled with the mingling scents of street food and the earthy aroma of morning dew. As the taxi left the city center, the scenery began to change dramatically. The road to the University of Petroleum and Energy Studies (UPES) curved through the verdant outskirts of the city, climbing gently into the foothills of the Himalayas. Kunal's eyes were glued to the window, captivated by the lush greenery that framed the winding road. Pine and deodar trees stood in stately rows, their branches whispering in the gentle mountain breeze. Every so often, the taxi passed small roadside shops displaying arrays of local handicrafts, from vibrant hand-woven shawls to intricately carved wooden artifacts, each telling a story of the region's rich cultural heritage.

As the taxi ascended higher, the air grew crisper, the backdrop more serene. The chaotic sounds of the city faded away, replaced by the tranquil sounds of nature—the chirping of birds and the rustling of leaves. The road meandered along the contour lines of the hills, offering glimpses of the valley below where streams flowed like ribbons of silver, catching the sunlight and glittering brightly against the dense green. The contrast between the town's bustling market areas and the tranquil, expansive greenery leading up to UPES was stark. The closer they got to the university, the more the landscape opened up, revealing sprawling fields dotted with wildflowers and occasional clusters of cottages. The architecture of the university began to peek through the foliage, modern structures with clean lines that contrasted beautifully with the natural ruggedness of the hills.

As the taxi turned into the main gate of UPES, Kunal felt a surge of anticipation. The campus was a beautiful blend of innovation and tradition, where state-of-the-art facilities were nestled amidst natural beauty, designed to inspire students and faculty alike. The pathways were lined with flowering bushes, and students from various disciplines traversed the campus, their youthful energy and enthusiastic chatter adding life to the serene environment. Kunal paid the taxi driver, grabbed his bags, and stepped out. With each step, his excitement built. Here, surrounded by the inspiring beauty of nature and the buzz of academic pursuit, Kunal felt a deep sense of possibility. This was where he would chase his dreams, surrounded by minds as eager and ambitious as his own.

As Kunal stepped through the gates of the University of Petroleum and Energy Studies (UPES), his eyes were immediately drawn to the stunning architecture that blended modern design with elements of traditional Indian artistry. The main building, with its sweeping curves and expansive glass facades, reflected the bright morning light, casting shimmering patterns on the paved walkway. Surrounding this central structure were various other buildings, each showcasing innovative design, with green rooftops and solar panels that spoke of the university's commitment to sustainability. The campus was alive with the buzz of student activities. Groups of students lounged on grassy knolls, some poring over textbooks, others animatedly discussing their projects. The air was filled with a blend of languages and accents, highlighting the diversity of the student body. Kunal noticed a group of engineering students huddled around a drone, making adjustments to its design, while a few yards away, art students sketched the natural scenery that the campus offered. As Kunal walked towards the administrative building to finalize his registration, he was approached by a senior student, recognizable by the university badge pinned prominently on her blazer.

"First year?" she asked with a friendly smile, her eyes twinkling with a mix of curiosity and welcoming warmth. "Yes," Kunal replied, slightly taken aback by her directness but grateful for the interaction. "I'm Ayesha, third year in Applied Petroleum Engineering. You look a bit lost, can I help you find your way?" she offered, her voice as warm as the morning sun. "Actually, yes. I need to get to the administrative office," Kunal said, feeling a sense of relief wash over him. "Follow me, I'm headed in that direction. Welcome to UPES! You'll love it here," Ayesha said, leading the way. As they walked, she pointed out various landmarks: the library known for its extensive collection of energy sector publications, the student café famous for its coffee and late-night debates, and the innovation lab where students worked on cutting-edge projects that often turned into real-world solutions.

Kunal soaked in every detail, his initial apprehension giving way to excitement. The vibrant energy of the campus, the blend of academic rigor, and the casual camaraderie among students—all of it felt invigorating. This was a place where he could see himself thriving, pushing boundaries, and perhaps, finding his own path. They reached the administrative building, a structure as impressive as the others, with large, welcoming doors and a facade adorned with murals depicting various aspects of student life at UPES. "Here we are," Ayesha said, stopping at the entrance. "You'll need your admission letter and some ID. Don't hesitate to join the orientation activities, and if you have any questions, everyone here is pretty helpful." "Thank you, Ayesha. Really appreciate the help," Kunal thanked her, his nervousness replaced by a budding confidence. "No problem! See you around campus!" Ayesha waved goodbye and disappeared into the crowd.

Stepping into the administrative office to sort out his paperwork, Kunal felt ready. Whatever challenges lay ahead, he was now on his path, eager and open to everything his new life at college would offer.

ᐅᐅᐅ

3
Settling In

Stepping into the spacious, brightly lit administrative office, Kunal was immediately struck by the vibrant atmosphere. The walls, adorned with accolades and interspersed with inspirational quotes from renowned leaders, conveyed the university's prestigious reputation. Around him, new students buzzed with excitement, filling out forms and waiting their turns at the counters, which added to the dynamic energy of the space.

Kunal approached the main desk, where he was greeted by a staff member with a friendly demeanor. Her name tag read "Mrs. Swati Verma." "Welcome! How can I assist you today?" she inquired, her tone both professional and inviting. "I'm here to complete my registration and pick up my orientation materials," Kunal replied, presenting his admission letter and identification. Mrs. Verma nodded and quickly retrieved his details from the system. "Ah, you're joining our MBA program—a wonderful choice. Our business school is highly acclaimed," she commented while printing out several documents. As Kunal filled out the necessary paperwork, Mrs. Verma explained each form with clarity. He signed his enrollment confirmation, received his student ID, and was handed a welcome kit containing a campus map, the academic calendar, and a student handbook.

"Your orientation begins tomorrow in the auditorium. It's an excellent chance to connect with your professors and classmates.

Also, make sure to join the campus tour afterward—it will help you get your bearings," Mrs. Verma advised, her eyes reflecting a warm, nostalgic glow. "Thank you, Mrs. Verma. I appreciate your help," Kunal said, organizing his documents neatly in his backpack. "You're welcome, Mr. Sharma. And remember, I'm here if you need any help during your stay," she responded, giving him a reassuring smile. Feeling more prepared and a little relieved now that the administrative tasks were behind him, Kunal left the office ready to embrace his new life. His next task was to find his hostel and settle into his room. He navigated through the campus pathways, each turn revealing a bit more of the vibrant student life and scenic beauty that the university had to offer.

Upon arriving at the hostel, Kunal checked in at the front desk where he was given his room key and directions. His room was on the third floor, overlooking a small garden that was part of the hostel's common area. Walking into the room, he was pleased to find it clean and spacious, with two beds, two desks, and a large window that let in plenty of natural light. He began unpacking his belongings, arranging his books, clothes, and personal items. Setting up his study space, he placed his laptop, notebooks, and a few favorite pens in an orderly fashion. As he organized, he thought about the coming days—starting classes, meeting new people, and diving into campus life.

Just as he finished unpacking, the door swung open and in walked a young man with an easy smile and an outstretched hand. "Hey! You must be Kunal. I'm Siddharth, your roommate, also a fresher here," he introduced himself warmly. "Nice to meet you, Siddharth," Kunal responded, shaking his hand. They spent a few minutes chatting about their courses, hometowns, and interests. It was clear from the start that they were going to get along well. With his room set up and a promising new friendship beginning, Kunal felt a growing excitement about the adventures that lay ahead. He knew there would be challenges, but he was ready to meet them head-on, supported by the new connections he was starting to forge.

Kunal and Siddharth stepped out into the early evening, eager to explore the sprawling campus of their new university home. The air was cool, with a light mist that clung to the lush landscape around them. As they approached the main gate, Kunal felt as if they had entered a scene straight from a vividly imagined movie. The clouds, heavy and low, skimmed the treetops and rooftops of nearby buildings, moving slowly and adding a touch of surreal beauty to the evening. "There's something magical about this place, isn't there?" Siddharth remarked, his eyes wide with wonder as they passed through the college gates.

To their right, just off the path, was an Oriental Bank ATM, a reminder of the world outside this secluded haven. But as they moved beyond the functional into the heart of the campus, every step revealed more of its breathtaking charm. The first building they encountered was a three-storied structure, old yet imposing, that seemed to guard the secrets of decades of scholarly pursuits. As they walked around the building, the full grandeur of the campus unfolded before them. The college was cradled by hilly, green mountains on three sides, creating an amphitheater of natural beauty that was awe-inspiring. In the center of a large quadrangle stood a statue of Mahatma Gandhi, gazing out serenely over the students who moved past him, busy with their youthful endeavors.

"Look over there!" Kunal pointed towards an unexpected piece of history—a decommissioned fighter jet, its metallic body gleaming slightly under the fading light, placed there as a tribute to ingenuity and courage. The friends wandered towards the large green field at the back of the campus, where the grass felt like velvet underfoot. They kicked off their shoes and stepped onto the soft turf, each blade of grass tickling their feet, enhancing the sense of enchantment that the place evoked. Behind the college, the land dipped sharply to reveal a stunning vista. About 800 feet below, a small water stream meandered through the valley, its gentle flow a quiet whisper in the distance. Near the edge of this precipice sat a quaint tea shop, its simple wooden structure offering a perfect vantage point over the idyllic scene.

"Let's grab a tea," Siddharth suggested, leading the way to the shop. They ordered two glasses of tea, and sitting there on the edge, sipping the warm, flavorful brew, they felt a profound peace settling around them. The clouds rolled in low, almost ethereal, as if they were an arm's reach away, blending with the mist that rose from the mountainsides. In this tranquil setting, the rains would often sweep through, as if they belonged there, nourishing the land and adding a rhythm to the natural symphony of sights and sounds. It was, Kunal thought, like stepping into one of those nursery drawings where every element of nature lived in harmony—a sun peeking from behind the mountains, a stream flowing beneath, and cattle grazing in the distance.

As the evening deepened, the setting became even more magical, with the low clouds swirling around them, almost inviting them to reach out and touch the vaporous veil. It was a place where reality merged with dreams, and every sight, every sound, and every scent was a reminder of how nature's beauty could transcend the ordinary, turning a simple walk into an unforgettable exploration of a dreamlike landscape. "This," Kunal said, his voice low and full of awe, "is going to be an incredible chapter of our lives." Siddharth nodded in agreement, the fading light casting long shadows across their faces, but the glow in their eyes was unmistakable—they were exactly where they were meant to be. Refreshed from their tea and the serenity of the landscape, Kunal and Siddharth continued their exploration of the campus, each step unveiling a new facet of their college life. The cool air seemed to energize them, and with each breath, they felt more a part of this vibrant academic community.

They made their way to the sports facilities next. The university boasted an impressive array of athletic resources, including a swimming pool, a well-equipped gym, and most importantly for them, a pristine basketball court. As they approached the court, they saw a team practice in full swing, the players' energetic movements and the rhythmic bouncing of the ball creating a lively atmosphere that resonated with both Kunal and Siddharth. "Man, I can't wait to get on the court," Kunal said, his eyes lighting up with excitement.

It was well known that he had been a key player in his high school basketball team. "Me too. I played all through high school. Looks like we'll be teammates here as well," Siddharth replied, matching Kunal's enthusiasm. Both of them felt a renewed surge of energy, imagining themselves joining the university basketball team and contributing to its success.

Continuing the exploration, they headed to the university library. The impressive building stood at the heart of the academic sector, its grand façade promising a world of knowledge inside. As they stepped through the large entryway, the distinctive scent of books—old paper and binding glue—filled the air, a familiar comfort to any student. Siddharth's face brightened immediately, his steps quickening with excitement. "Wow, look at all these books! This place is a goldmine for research and learning. Can you imagine all the late nights we're going to spend here cramming for exams?" He wandered down an aisle, running his fingers along the spines of books, clearly enchanted by the scholarly atmosphere. Kunal, trailing behind, gave a half-smile. His gaze drifted more towards the layout and the exits than the books themselves. "Yeah, it's nice and big. Great for group studies or maybe a quiet nap between classes," he joked, more attuned to the practical uses of the space rather than its academic treasures. His mind was still back at the basketball court they had visited earlier, imagining the games and practices to come. Siddharth chuckled, pulling a book off the shelf. "You're going to love the study areas upstairs. They say you can see the entire campus from the top floor—it's perfect for some quiet time after a game when you need to switch gears and hit the books." Kunal nodded, appreciating Siddharth's attempt to bridge their different interests. "I'll definitely need some peace after practice. It's good to know there's a spot here where I can cool down and focus." They continued their tour of the library, with Siddharth pointing out various features like the digital research stations, private study rooms, and extensive online databases. Kunal listened, genuinely impressed by his roommate's knowledge and enthusiasm, though his main interest lay elsewhere. Their library visit wrapped up with

Siddharth more excited about the academic opportunities, while Kunal was already planning their next visit to the sports complex. It was clear they had different passions, but their mutual respect and growing friendship suggested they would navigate university life as a strong team.

Finally, they next visited the cafeteria, a lively hub of student activity. The space was bustling, filled with the chatter of students and the clinking of cutlery. The smell of freshly brewed coffee and a variety of cuisines filled the air, making Kunal's stomach rumble. They grabbed some snacks—a couple of samosas and cold drinks—and sat down to watch the ebb and flow of student life around them. "This place feels alive, doesn't it?" Kunal remarked, taking a bite of his samosa. "It's the heart of the campus," Siddharth agreed, his eyes scanning the crowd for familiar faces from their batch. Their last stop of the evening was the innovation lab, known for fostering student projects and startups. The lab was a creative space filled with the latest technology, including 3D printers, high-end computing resources, and prototype development tools. Students were busy at work, their faces illuminated by the soft glow of computer screens, discussing projects that ranged from sustainable energy solutions to software apps.

"Look at that," Kunal pointed to a group working on a drone, their focused expressions reflecting the intensity of their work. "We definitely need to check out some projects here; might even start our own," Siddharth said, his tone full of aspiration. As it started getting darker, the campus lights began to flicker on, casting long shadows and bathing the paths in a warm glow. The tour had given them a taste of what to expect in their university life, and both Kunal and Siddharth felt a growing excitement about the opportunities ahead. They walked back to their hostel, talking about the clubs they would join and the initiatives they might start. It was clear that their journey at the university would be about more than just academics—it would be about growth, learning, and making a tangible impact.

After their campus tour, Kunal and Siddharth returned to their room and found a mysterious note slipped under their door. It read, "Emergency meeting for all freshmen. Midnight at the old auditorium. This is a mandatory tradition." Signed simply, "The Committee." Feeling a mix of excitement and nervousness, they decided to head to the auditorium at midnight. As they approached the designated spot, they noticed other freshmen from various rooms also converging, all drawn by similar notes. The group, looking equally puzzled and anxious, introduced themselves and waited together outside the darkened entrance of the auditorium, the oldest and most legendary part of the university, known for its architecture and eerie tales.

The path was dimly lit, winding through ancient oaks that cast long, spooky shadows, enhancing the chilling ambiance of their walk. As the clock struck midnight, the air grew colder, and an unnatural fog began to settle around the base of the tower. The door to the auditorium creaked open slowly as they approached, revealing only darkness inside. Taking deep breaths and steeling themselves, the group stepped in, their footsteps echoing in the silent, vast space. Suddenly, a series of ghostly lights appeared, and eerie sounds echoed through the tower—a mix of whispers and soft, haunting melodies. The Kunal and Siddharth instinctively moved closer together, their initial fear turning into a cautious curiosity. Just as they were about to retreat, a figure draped in a flowing, spectral cloak floated towards them. The group jumped back, ready to run, when the figure suddenly burst into laughter, throwing off the cloak to reveal a group of seniors with grins plastered across their faces, holding small speakers and flashlights.

"Welcome to the Auditorium Bash, freshmen!" shouted one of the seniors, as more lights came on and music started playing. "You should see your faces!" The seniors explained that this "haunted" initiation was a prank to welcome new students and test their courage. It was all in good fun, and now the freshmen were truly part of the university family. They had passed the test by sticking together through the scare, proving they could rely on each other.

Kunal and Siddharth couldn't help but laugh along, relieved and amused by the turn of events. They joined the impromptu party that followed, with the seniors sharing stories of past pranks and traditions. This unexpected adventure not only broke the ice but also cemented the beginning of a strong friendship among the freshmen, especially between Kunal and Siddharth, as they realized they could indeed have each other's backs in unexpected situations.

After the laughs, shrieks and jump scares, the evening wound down with Kunal and Siddharth reflecting on their first day at university. They both agreed that, beyond the academics and the impressive campus, it was the people they met who made their new adventure truly exciting. "Looks like it's not just the basketball court where we'll be scoring points," Siddharth quipped as they prepared for bed. "Definitely, this is just the beginning," Kunal said, a wide smile spreading across his face. "Exactly," Siddharth replied, "And it's going to be epic!"

4

Challenges, Triumphs and… Sakshi

The sun had barely crested the horizon, casting a soft golden light over the campus as Kunal hurried along the path to his first MBA lecture. The crisp morning air did little to calm his fluttering nerves. Today wasn't just another day; it was the beginning of his journey into the complex world of business strategy. He entered the large auditorium where his Strategic Management class was to be held. Students from diverse backgrounds filled the room, their murmurs echoing off the high ceilings, creating a buzz of anticipatory energy. Kunal found a seat in the middle row, strategically chosen to ensure a perfect balance between visibility and engagement. Beside him, Siddharth, equally eager and a bit apprehensive, shared a nod of mutual encouragement.

The lecture began with the arrival of Professor Arora, who was as formidable in reputation as she was in intellect. With a commanding presence, she greeted the class and launched straight into the intricacies of business environments and the importance of strategic thinking in modern corporations. Kunal, pen poised over his notebook, found himself initially overwhelmed by the rapid pace and depth of information. The theories were complex, intertwined with real-world applications that demanded a keen understanding and critical thinking. As he struggled to keep up, noting down as much as he could, he realized this was a different ballgame from his undergraduate studies.

About midway through the session, Professor Arora called for a class discussion on a case study. Siddharth, feeling somewhat prepared, raised his hand to contribute. His voice faltered slightly as he began, his argument not as polished as he had hoped. A few classmates looked puzzled, and Siddharth could feel a slight heat creeping up his neck. Kunal, seeing his friend's discomfort, quickly chimed in with whatever bare minimum he remembered, supporting Siddharth's point with a supplementary insight that clarified their stance. After the class, as students filed out, Kunal and Siddharth approached Professor Arora, their steps hesitant but determined. "Professor, I had some trouble following some of the concepts today," Siddharth admitted, his voice betraying his frustration.

Professor Arora looked at them, her expression serious yet kind. "It's a common initial reaction. MBA courses are designed to push you, to expand your way of thinking," she explained, her tone encouraging. "Keep engaging with the material, and don't hesitate to seek help or clarification. You're not alone in this journey." Kunal and Siddharth spent extra hours in the library that week despite Kunal throwing a fit about it. While he wanted to be out playing basketball, Siddharth made them both join study groups, and engage in online forums. Each day brought a little more clarity, and slowly, the puzzle pieces began to fit together. They started preparing questions in advance, actively participating in discussions, and their contributions began gaining recognition from both peers and professors.

As weeks turned into months, the academic challenges that had once seemed daunting now energized Kunal and Siddharth. They found themselves thriving in the rigorous environment, pushing their boundaries, and delighting in the intellectual growth they experienced. The fears and uncertainties of the first few classes faded into a confident pursuit of knowledge, marked by a keen understanding and a critical approach to complex business strategies. By mid-semester, they were not only keeping up with their classes but excelling in them. The initial setbacks had transformed into stepping stones, and they looked forward to each new lecture as an opportunity to stretch their capabilities further. Their relationship with Professor Arora also grew; she became a mentor, guiding them through the nuances of business management with a firm yet supportive hand. Kunal grumbled and whined about having to put in an extra hour of studies, but Siddharth managed to coax him and got him to tag along for every study session.

As Kunal and Siddharth walked out of the auditorium after a particularly stimulating lecture on competitive dynamics, they couldn't help but feel grateful for the challenges that had pushed them to evolve. The academic journey was indeed rigorous, but it was also incredibly rewarding, and they were determined to make the most of every lesson learned. In the weeks that followed, Kunal's reputation among his classmates began to flourish, not only as a friendly and charming person but also due to the unique blend of his poetic nature with the cutthroat business environment of his MBA classes. Often, during breaks or in more casual settings like the campus café, Kunal would share verses he had written, reflections inspired by his lectures or the natural beauty of the campus. His words, infused with thoughtfulness and a touch of vulnerability, resonated with many, creating a bridge between him and his peers.

One afternoon, after a particularly challenging case study discussion, Kunal sat under the shade of a large oak tree on the green lawn outside the library. With a notebook on his lap, he scribbled lines, weaving his reflections on the day's lessons with the serene landscape around him. Siddharth, who had become not only a roommate but a confidant, joined him, along with a few other classmates who had begun to appreciate Kunal's lyrical insights. "Hey, what are you writing today?" asked Rizwan, as he took a seat beside them. His interest in Kunal's poetry had grown after he had shared a piece which beautifully captured the beauty of nature. Kunal smiled, closing his notebook gently. "Just some random thoughts. Trying to capture the essence of life through my words," he replied, his eyes lighting up with enthusiasm.

"Would you mind sharing it with us?" another classmate, Arjun, chimed in. The group around them nodded in agreement, curious to hear his latest creation. With a slight nod, Kunal opened his notebook and began to read. His voice was calm, almost meditative, as he recited:

She was the girl of passion and pride,
Shining brighter than the brightest light.
The clock took a turn and showed its side,
Causing her to lose her bravest knight.
She walks alone in the darkest night,
Finding her way under the moon's bright light.
    Things have changed, and time has passed,
People want her to grasp every lesson cast.
So she transformed in her own way,
Carrying burdens in her heart each day,
Yet you'd always see her with a smile so wide,
For she is a girl of passion and pride.

As Kunal finished, a soft applause broke out among his friends, appreciative of the way he could distill complex ideas into poignant, accessible verse. "That was amazing, Kunal," Rizwan said, his expression one of genuine admiration. "You have a real gift." "Thanks, Rizwan. I find that it helps me process everything that goes on around me better," Kunal confessed. "Sharing it is just a bonus." As the semester progressed, these small poetry sessions became a regular occurrence, not only helping Kunal connect with his peers but also allowing him to maintain his passion for poetry amidst the rigors of his MBA studies. It was in these moments that Kunal truly shined, his poetic expressions becoming as much a part of his identity as his analytical skills.

These interactions, layered with academic collaboration and the shared struggles of navigating a demanding MBA program, solidified friendships within the group. They were more than just classmates; they were fellow travelers on a journey of growth and discovery, each bringing their unique strengths and vulnerabilities to the collective table. Kunal's ability to blend poetry with business not only endeared him to his peers but also brought a unique perspective to his studies, proving that even in the most unlikely environments, art finds its space, enriching conversations and deepening understandings.

Sakshi, another MBA student, was setting her journey on a similar, ambitious path as Kunal. With dreams as high as the mountains that surrounded the campus, she had meticulously prepared for her tryst with MBA. Her initial weeks at college were a whirlwind of academics. Every waking moment seemed to be consumed by lectures, group projects, and an endless stream of assignments. The pressure to excel was immense, and though Sakshi was no stranger to hard work, the intensity of the MBA program began to weigh heavily on her. The joy of learning, which had always fueled her ambitions, was slowly being overshadowed by stress and frustration. One evening, after a particularly taxing day, Sakshi's roommate, Anjali, noticed her distress. "You look like you could use a break," her roommate commented, concern lacing her voice as she watched Sakshi pore over her books with furrowed brows.

Sakshi sighed, rubbing her temples. "I just don't understand why it's not clicking. I've been at this for hours." "Maybe that's the problem," Anjali suggested gently. "You've been so focused on studies that you've forgotten what it's like to have a bit of fun. What about your hobbies? You used to play basketball back home, right?" The mention of basketball sparked a flicker of light in Sakshi's eyes. "I did... I haven't even thought about it since I got here." "Why not pick it up again?" Anjali encouraged. "It could be a great way to unwind, and who knows, it might even help clear your mind."

Sakshi considered this. The idea of feeling the basketball in her hands again, the court under her feet, it was tempting. It reminded her of the balance she once had between her studies and her love for the game. Resolute, she decided to find a way to incorporate basketball into her routine, despite her packed schedule from 9:45 AM to 5:15 PM. It was time to reclaim a part of herself that was lost amidst the pursuit of academic excellence. The next day, Sakshi made her way to the university's sports complex. As she stepped onto the basketball court, a sense of familiarity washed over her. Picking up a ball, she dribbled down the court, the familiar thump of the ball against the hardwood a comforting rhythm that countered the chaos of her academic life. With each shot, her stress seemed to dissipate, melting away with the sweat that beaded on her forehead. She felt alive again, rejuvenated by reconnecting with her long-neglected passion.

Little did she know that it was on this court her path would eventually cross with Kunal's, their shared interests laying the groundwork for a friendship that would weave through the narrative of their MBA journey. But for now, Sakshi was content to lose herself in the game she loved, rediscovering the joy that had once defined her so completely. As the crisp autumn air settled over the campus, whispers of the upcoming basketball tryouts began to circulate among the students. Both Kunal and Sakshi, unbeknownst to each other, were drawn to the possibility of joining their respective college basketball teams. Their paths, paralleled by shared interests yet still unmet, were about to intersect on the courts.

The basketball court buzzed with anticipation as Kunal and Siddharth joined the throng of male students warming up, each one eager to showcase his skills and secure a place on the team. The sound of bouncing balls, squeaking sneakers, and the occasional whistle filled the air, setting a backdrop of serious competitive spirit. Kunal, despite his previous experience and love for the game, couldn't shake off a bout of nerves. His hands felt unusually clammy as he took his first practice shots, the rim seeming just a bit elusive. Siddharth, noticing his friend's anxiety, clapped him on the back, offering a grin. "Hey, just like our scrimmages back home, right? You got this," he encouraged. As the tryouts officially began, Kunal found his rhythm. Each pass, dribble, and shot started to feel more natural, his confidence building with every successful play. Siddharth, too, displayed his prowess, his agile moves and sharp shooting complementing Kunal's strategic playmaking. Together, they made a formidable duo, quickly catching the coach's eye.

On the adjacent court, Sakshi laced up her sneakers with a determination that steadied her shaking hands. The women's team tryouts were just as charged with energy, the air punctuated by the same intensity and excitement as the men's. Sakshi took a deep breath, channeling her nerves into focus. She joined the other hopefuls on the court, each dribble and shot a step towards proving she belonged on the team. Her skills, honed through years of practice, shone through. Her movements were fluid-like, her understanding of the game apparent in her positioning and decision-making. Each swish of the net added to her growing confidence, her initial nervousness fading into the background.

During a break in the men's tryouts, Kunal's gaze briefly shifted to the women's half of the court. Amidst the flurry of activity, one player stood out with her clear command of the game. Sakshi executed a perfect three-pointer, her form not just technically flawless but displaying an effortless mastery that caught Kunal's attention. Her presence on the court was not only about skill but also an evident passion for the game, which resonated with Kunal's own dedication to basketball. He noted her prowess, appreciating the seamless way she wove through her opponents, her focus sharp and unwavering. It was the kind of athletic excellence that demanded recognition, and Kunal, always keen to learn from watching others, briefly admired her play.

Yet, his mind quickly returned to his own performance. Today, nothing could distract him—not when every dribble, every pass, and every shot could mean the difference between securing a spot on the team or watching from the sidelines. His heart was set on one thing alone—earning his place on the team. The intense determination filled him, and he redirected his full attention back to the men's court. As he prepared for the next phase of the tryouts, his thoughts were only on the movements, strategies, and skills he needed to display. Sakshi's impressive gameplay was a fleeting thought, noted and appreciated, but secondary to the goal in front of him. "Focus, Kunal," he muttered to himself, bouncing the ball with renewed vigor. The gym's sounds, the coaches' calls, and his competitors' footsteps refocused him. Everything else faded into the background as he honed in on the basket in front of him.

5

Courtside Chronicles

The gymnasium was charged with an electric mix of nerves and anticipation as Kunal and Siddharth, alongside a throng of eager athletes, awaited the final team selections. The atmosphere was thick with hope and ambition, each player mentally rehearsing future plays. When the coach finally called out their names to confirm their spots on the men's basketball team, a loud cheer erupted from Kunal and Siddharth. Siddharth punched the air, his loud laughter drowning all the other sounds. Kunal meanwhile experienced a rush of adrenaline and felt a strong wave of anticipation wash over him.

Their excitement was visible as they joined the rest of the selected team members. Conversations quickly sparked up about strategies and potential plays they could use to outsmart their competitors. The energy in the group was contagious, everyone eager to contribute their ideas. "Hey Siddharth, I was thinking about using quick passes and sharp cuts to break through their defense," Kunal suggested, his eyes gleaming with enthusiasm. "Absolutely! And we can add some pick-and-rolls. I've been watching our rivals, and they rely heavily on zone defense. We could exploit that easily," Siddharth replied, equally enthusiastic. Arjun, one of their new teammates, chimed in. "I've seen some videos of our rivals. We need to work on our communication. If we can read each other's moves, we can break their defense before they even have a chance to react."

George nodded in agreement. "And we need to practice our fast breaks. Quick transitions can catch them off guard."

The group buzzed with ideas, each player bringing their unique perspective to the table. Despite not having played their first official match, their similarity in energy levels was evident. They came across as a formidable team. "Guys, I can already see us dominating the court with our combined skills and strategies. We're going to be unstoppable!" Siddharth said confidently. Meanwhile on the adjacent court, the women's team selections were also being finalized. The anticipation was just as high as names were called out. When Sakshi's name was announced, a deafening cheer erupted from her and her friends. Her face lit up with pride and joy.

Once the celebrations began to wind down, the head coaches of both the men's and women's basketball teams called for attention. The two coaches, Coach Rajan and Coach Anita, both former players with numerous championships under their belts, stood at the center of the gym. Coach Rajan addressed the gathering first. "Congratulations to each one of you selected today," he said with authority and warmth. "Being a member of this team is more than just about playing basketball. It's about building character, discipline, and a sense of community. We're not just a team; we're a family, and every practice, every game, is a step towards greater achievements together." Coach Anita continued, her tone equally inspiring. "This season, our target should be to achieve what the previous teams have failed to achieve so far. Each of you has shown exceptional skill and potential, and it's our job to harness that into a cohesive force on the court. We expect commitment, hard work, and most importantly, support for one another."

She then announced, "Our first official practice session starts tomorrow at 5:30 PM, right after classes. This season is about pushing our limits and justifying your selection in this team." The room burst into applause, the players' faces lit up with renewed vigor and anticipation. As Kunal left the gym, the cool evening air did little to temper the warmth blooming in his chest, fueled by the thrill of making the team and the possibility of playing the finals of the upcoming tournament. Kunal, Sid and the rest of the team kept yapping excitedly about playing all along the way to their rooms, their excitement reaching a fever pitch.

It was the day of the first official basketball practice and Kunal was unusually restless as the final class of the day dragged on. The day had been particularly draining, filled with back-to-back lectures, group discussions, and multiple PowerPoint presentations. His brain was muddled with concepts and deadlines, making it hard to stay focused. Typically attentive and engaged, today he was distracted, his gaze often drifting to the clock above the door, counting down the minutes. The anticipation of hitting the court and getting some relief from the intense academic pressure made it nearly impossible for him to focus on the professor's lecture.

Siddharth, seated next to him, leaned over and whispered, "You okay? You've checked the time more in the last hour than you have all semester." Kunal offered a sheepish grin, trying to mask his impatience. "Just looking forward to the practice," he murmured, though his eyes darted away, clearly eager for the physical activity to break the monotony of the day. Siddharth chuckled, seeing right through his friend's casual dismissal. "Yeah, I hear you. This day has been brutal," he said, nudging Kunal playfully. Finally, as the class ended, Kunal quickly gathered his things, his movements swift and a bit more hurried than usual. They headed to the gym where both the teams were already assembling and had begun stretching to gear up for the session. The atmosphere was vibrant, filled with the sounds of bouncing basketballs and energetic chatter.

The practise session kicked off with a series of dynamic warm-ups which had everyone moving in sync to perform jumping jacks, sprint drills, and agility ladders. The energy in the gym was infectious, each player feeding off the collective drive and focus. As they moved into more specialized drills, Kunal once again noticed Sakshi's moves. He was impressed with how effortlessly she moved around the court with speed and agility. Coaches Rajan and Anita were actively involved throughout the drills, their expertise evident as they provided guidance and adjustments to the players' techniques. "Good form, Siddharth! Keep those passes sharp!" Coach Rajan called out, his voice resonating across the gym. He made his way through the players, pausing to offer tips on shooting and defense, his keen eyes missing nothing.

Coach Anita, on the other hand, was focused on the positioning and movement, often pulling aside players to demonstrate better footwork or positioning. "Sakshi, that's an excellent drive to the basket, but let's work on your finishing," she advised, showing her the optimal angle for layups. As Siddharth and Kunal paired up for a passing drill, their natural chemistry as forwards became immediately apparent. Despite never having played on the same team before, their understanding of each other's movements was instinctual, a testament to their years of playing at their schools but mastering similar positions. Their passes were fluid, and their coordinated attacks during the scrimmage portion of the practice drew nods of approval from both coaches.

"Watch those two," Coach Rajan pointed out to a group of newer players, referring to Kunal and Siddharth. "That's the kind of awareness and teamwork we want to build here." The practice then transitioned into a scrimmage, a mock match to put their skills to the test. Kunal and Siddharth were a formidable duo on the court, their passes and plays almost telepathic. Sakshi, who was displaying impressive prowess in the women's scrimmage alongside her teammates caught Coach Anita's attention as well. Her strategic plays were impossible for her not to appreciate. When their exercises aligned very now and then, Kunal's and Sakshi's paths would cross on the court. But they were so focussed on the practise that they never really spoke or interacted beyond a 'hey' or an 'excuse me'.

As the session wrapped up, the gym was abuzz with the sounds of heavy breathing and the thud of basketballs being racked. Coaches Rajan and Anita gathered everyone for a quick debrief, praising the effort and pointing out areas for improvement. "Great energy today, everyone. Remember, this is just the beginning. We build from here," Coach Anita said, her voice encouraging. The coaches asked for everyone's attention to make one final announcement. The players huddled around, still catching their breath and wiping sweat from their brows, their eyes fixed on the coaches with anticipation. "Before we break," Coach Rajan started, his voice firm yet imbued with a sense of pride, "we have one more important piece of business. Leadership on the court is crucial, and after careful consideration, we've made our decisions for this season's team captains."

There was a palpable pause, the air thick with suspense. "For the men's team, we've chosen someone who has not only demonstrated exceptional skill but also a natural ability to motivate and lead—Siddharth." A cheer erupted from the team as Siddharth's face lit up with a mix of surprise and excitement. He stepped forward, shaking hands with Coach Rajan, his smile broad and confident. Simultaneously, Coach Anita addressed the women's team. "And for our women's team, we need a leader who embodies dedication, skill, and sportsmanship. This season, Sakshi will take on that role." Sakshi, equally surprised and honored, nodded her acceptance, her eyes scanning her teammates who were now applauding and cheering her on.

After the announcement, as the teams dispersed slightly, Siddharth approached Sakshi to introduce himself as her male counterpart. "Looks like we'll be leading together," he said with a friendly grin, extending his hand. Sakshi shook his hand warmly. "I'm looking forward to it. Seems like we have a great season ahead," she responded, her voice reflecting a mix of determination and enthusiasm. They quickly delved into a light-hearted discussion about their strategies and thoughts on leadership, laughing over shared challenges they anticipated. Their easy rapport was evident, making it clear they would work well together. Meanwhile, Kunal waited on the sidelines for Sid, packing his sports bag while taking sips of an energy drink.

When Siddharth returned, Kunal asked, "How's Sakshi? She seems competent." Siddharth, ever the prankster, decided to tease Kunal. "Oh, she's more than competent. Really cool and pretty sharp with her plays. You should talk to her sometime, Kunal. You two would get along," he nudged, winking. Kunal's rolled his eyes, brushing off his friend's insinuation that he might be interested in Sakshi. He made a face and changed the subject, "Yeah, maybe. We should focus on those drills Coach mentioned first, right?" His attempt to divert the conversation was transparent, causing Siddharth to laugh outright. "Sure, man. Whatever you say," Siddharth chuckled, patting Kunal on the back as they walked off the court together, their conversation turning back to basketball. His mind replayed the day's practices, excited about the next day of practise. Kunal, Siddharth, and a few of their new teammates made their way to the hostel mess, their stomachs roaring loudly after their intense practise session. The mess hall buzzed with the chatter of students, the clatter of trays, and the occasional laugh that cut through the din.

The aroma of dinner wafted through the air, a comforting blend of spices and warmth. Tonight's menu featured chapatis, dal tadka, vegetable biryani, and warm gulab jamuns for dessert that promised a sweet end to the day. The players loaded their trays, the piles of food seemingly a reflection of their day's hard work. As they settled at a long table, the conversation flowed as freely as the food on their plates. Between mouthfuls, they exchanged stories from their various hometowns, discussed favorite NBA teams, and recounted first impressions of college life. Siddharth, always the more outspoken, animatedly described some of their more humorous missteps during practice, drawing hearty laughs from around the table. Kunal joined in with his own quips, though his focus was on the food in front of him!

After dinner, as they strolled back to their hostel, Kunal's phone rang. It was his mother, checking in as she often did. "Hi, Ma," Kunal greeted, his voice carrying a mix of fatigue and contentment. "Kunal, how was your day? Did you eat properly?" Her questions came quick, filled with the usual maternal concern. "It was great, Ma. Just had dinner. You won't believe how much Siddharth can eat," Kunal replied, laughing as he glanced at Siddharth, who took the phone from him, eager to join the conversation. "Hello, Auntie! Yes, I'm making sure he eats well and stays out of trouble," Siddharth chimed in, his voice cheerful. The sound of his mother's laughter came through the phone, pleased with Siddharth's assurance. "Make sure both of you look after each other. And Kunal, your dad and I are so proud to hear you made the basketball team! Tell us more about it," she continued, her voice brimming with pride.

Kunal took the phone back, his chest swelling a bit with pride. "It's exciting, Ma. The coaches are great, and I'm learning a lot already. And guess what? Siddharth is the captain of the team!" "Oh, that's wonderful! We're so happy for you boys. Make sure you keep up with your studies too," she advised, ever the pragmatic parent. "We will, Ma. Thanks," Kunal reassured her, feeling a warmth that only a call home could provide. As they reached their hostel, Kunal ended the call with promises to visit soon, his spirits lifted by his family's support and the camaraderie of his new life at college.

6

On-Court Glory, Off-Court Bonds

As the date of the inter-college basketball tournament drew near, UPES was abuzz with excitement and anticipation. Both the men's and women's basketball teams were undergoing intense training sessions under the vigilant eyes of their coaches, Rajan and Anita. The grueling practice sessions were designed not just to refine their skills but also to build stamina and team synergy, critical for the upcoming challenges.

The gymnasium echoed with the sounds of bouncing basketballs, squeaking sneakers, and the occasional whistle that marked the start or end of a drill. Kunal, alongside Siddharth, pushed himself to the limits, his body drenched in sweat as he executed play after play. Each session ended with strategic meetings where Coach Rajan discussed tactics and plays that could give them an edge in the tournament. Sakshi, leading the women's team, was equally involved in rigorous training sessions. Her leadership shone as she motivated her team, ensuring every member was in sync and ready for what lay ahead. Her dedication and skill were evident in each practice, earning her nods of approval from Coach Anita, who often praised her for her sharp game sense and ability to inspire her teammates.

As the tournament commenced, the atmosphere at UPES was electric. Banners fluttered in the gentle breeze, and the stands were filled with students, faculty, and visitors, all eager to support their teams. The tournament was officially opened with a speech by the university's dean, emphasizing sportsmanship and the honor of hosting such a prestigious event. The men's team, with Kunal and Siddharth at the forefront, showcased a spectacular performance from the very first match. Their seamless coordination and strategic gameplay allowed them to dominate their opponents, securing a series of wins that propelled them through the rounds. Kunal's prowess on the court didn't go unnoticed, his swift movements and accurate shooting garnering cheers from the crowd, especially during a critical semi-final match where his crucial baskets in the dying minutes helped secure a victory for his team.

Parallelly, the women's team, led by Sakshi, displayed remarkable skill and determination. Sakshi's leadership was palpable, her calls and setups on the court guiding her team through tough matches. Her performance was especially stellar during the semi-finals, where she led by example, scoring the highest points and steering her team to a hard-fought win. As both teams made it to the finals, the excitement reached a fever pitch. Throughout the tournament, Kunal and Sakshi's paths crossed several times, their interactions brief yet filled with mutual respect and admiration.

As the day of the finals dawned, the UPES campus transformed into a vibrant hub of festivity and anticipation. The usually serene walkways buzzed with excitement as students and faculty alike geared up for the climactic showdowns of the basketball tournament. Banners in vibrant hues of blue and gold, the university's colors, were strung across the main quadrangles and along the paths leading to the gymnasium. Each banner featured the faces of the key players, including action shots of Kunal and Sakshi, with slogans like "Aim High, Fly Higher" and "Courage Under Fire" emblazoned across them. The images stirred a sense of pride and unity among the spectators, creating a palpable sense of belonging and shared ambition. Student volunteers, identifiable by their spirited attire and badges, were busy setting up public viewing areas with large projectors and seating arrangements. These zones quickly became gathering points, where groups of students came together, some dressed in the team's merchandise, discussing strategies and player forms with a fervor typically reserved for professional leagues.

Near the gymnasium, the atmosphere was even more electric. Food stalls had been set up, serving everything from hot dogs and nachos to local delicacies like samosas and chai, turning the area into a mini festival. Music played in the background, a mix of upbeat tracks and college anthems, adding to the carnival-like atmosphere. Faculty members were not left behind in the excitement. Many donned the university's sports gear and could be seen mingling with students, sharing their own college sports experiences, and offering words of encouragement. It wasn't just a display of support for the basketball teams but a celebration of the university's community spirit.

Inside the gymnasium, the stands were decorated with balloons and streamers, and a large banner reading "Go UPES, Win the Trophy!" hung prominently behind the scorer's table. The seating was quickly filling up, with students, alumni, and local sports enthusiasts eager to witness the showdown. As the teams warmed up on the court, the cheerleading squad took to the sidelines, rehearsing their routines and cheers, their pom-poms glinting in the team colors under the gym lights. Their energy was infectious, pulling even the most reserved spectators into the wave of enthusiasm that swept through the venue.

Every slam of the ball on the court, every swish of the net, and every cheer from the crowd built a crescendo of anticipation that echoed across the campus. It was more than just a game; it was a culmination of hard work, dreams, and the unyielding spirit of a community that thrived on excellence and unity. This festive, almost electric atmosphere not only heightened the excitement for the final games but also knit the community closer, turning the day into a memorable celebration of sportsmanship and collegiate pride. The finals of the inter-college basketball tournament were not just a test of skill but a showcase of the determination and spirit honed over the season. The gym was packed, the air thick with anticipation and the roaring support of the crowd, as the UPES men's and women's teams prepared for their respective final matches.

The men's team faced a formidable opponent known for their aggressive defense and sharpshooters. The game started intensely, with both teams exchanging leads in the first few quarters. Kunal, under the vigilant leadership of Siddharth, was pivotal in breaking through the opposing team's defense. His agility and precision on the court allowed him to weave past defenders and make crucial baskets, keeping the score tight. As the final quarter began, UPES was trailing by a few points. The atmosphere was tense, with the crowd on the edge of their seats. Coach Rajan called a timeout, gathering the team for a quick strategy discussion. "We need to tighten our defense and look for quick breaks," he instructed, focusing on exploiting the opponent's slower transitions. Resuming play, Siddharth executed a series of plays that demonstrated why he was the captain. With a calm demeanor and sharp eye, he orchestrated the team's movements, setting up Kunal for critical shots. Kunal, seizing each opportunity, scored two consecutive three-pointers, shifting the momentum in their favor.

The defense tightened up as instructed, with team members blocking and intercepting passes. In the final minutes, with UPES now leading, the opponent tried to push back hard, but the defense held strong. As the buzzer sounded, the scoreline favored UPES, the gym erupted in cheers and applause. The team embraced, their faces a mixture of relief and joy, celebrating a hard-fought victory that crowned them champions. Parallelly, the women's team, led by Sakshi, displayed exceptional teamwork and strategy. Sakshi's role as captain was evident as she rallied her team, maintaining their focus and boosting their morale throughout the game. The women's final was a clash of tactics, with both teams showcasing excellent defensive and offensive plays.

Sakshi was a whirlwind on the court, maneuvering past defenses and assisting in crucial plays. Her ability to read the game and make split-second decisions made her a formidable leader. Midway through, the game was evenly matched, with neither team giving an inch. During a brief timeout, Kunal, observing the women's game from the sidelines, noticed a pattern in the opponent's play. One of the players, who excelled in fast-breaks, was often left unmarked and was scoring most of their points. Kunal quickly approached Coach Anita and shared his observation, suggesting a man-to-man defense to curb her scoring. Coach Anita nodded, appreciating the keen insight, and relayed the strategy to Sakshi. In the second half, Sakshi's strategic acumen came to the forefront.

She incorporated Kunal's suggestion, assigning a player to tightly mark the fast-break specialist. This adjustment caused turnovers that led to vital points for her team. Her leadership shone brightest in the final quarter, where she took control, scoring several key points and setting up her teammates. Her efforts culminated in a decisive play where she stole the ball and passed it to a teammate, who scored the winning basket. As the final whistle blew, the women's team erupted in celebration, their victory a testament to their hard work, unity, and the leadership of Sakshi. They joined the men's team in jubilation, the dual victories amplifying the festive atmosphere. The triumph of the tournament was fresh, the celebrations euphoric, when Coach Rajan and Coach Anita decided to take both the men's and women's basketball teams out for a celebratory dinner. The venue was a cozy local restaurant known for its hearty cuisine and warm ambiance, perfect for the teams to unwind and enjoy their success together.

As they settled into the rustic, wooden booths of the restaurant, the atmosphere was light and filled with laughter. Players chatted animatedly, their conversations a mix of game recaps and plans for the upcoming semester. Kunal, still riding the high of their victory, found himself a bit more reserved. Siddharth, ever observant of his friend's shifting moods, steered Kunal to sit at a booth that was coincidentally (or so Siddharth claimed) next to where Sakshi and some of her teammates had gathered. Kunal's initial instinct was to make an excuse and move to another seat, but Siddharth, with a mischievous grin, firmly patted him on the shoulder, signaling him to stay put.

As luck—or perhaps fate—would have it, Sakshi glanced over just then, her eyes meeting Kunal's with a spark of recognition that seemed to light up her features. "Hey, Kunal," she greeted warmly, her voice carrying a melody that Kunal felt resonated right to his core. "Congratulations again on the win. You played amazingly." Kunal, momentarily lost for words, managed a smile. "Thanks, Sakshi. You were incredible out there too. Watching you lead was... inspiring." Their conversation, though simple, was laden with the undercurrents of a budding connection. As they spoke of the upcoming class projects and their favorite spots on campus to study or relax, it was clear they were deeply engrossed in each other's company. The rest of the team moved around the restaurant, grabbing mocktails and more food, their laughter and chatter creating a lively background. But Kunal and Sakshi stayed rooted to their spots, completely absorbed in their conversation. Sakshi's friends, including Anjali, noticed the pair's growing rapport but chose to keep quiet, exchanging knowing glances and smiling discreetly. They intended to bring it up later in their hostel, teasing Sakshi about her new friend.

Throughout their exchange, Siddharth made it a point to walk by their booth under various pretenses: grabbing extra napkins, fetching condiments, each time shooting Kunal a teasing look or a dramatically raised eyebrow that had Kunal shaking his head in a blend of embarrassment and amusement. Despite his friend's antics, Kunal felt a warmth spreading through him that had little to do with the bustling atmosphere of the restaurant. And for the first time, Kunal noticed how beautiful Sakshi was. Her light brown eyes, hair that barely touched her shoulders and an athletic figure that struck the perfect balance between slim and curvy. For a second, he was lost in her beauty before being brought back to focus by her voice. They discussed their hobbies, Kunal shared his passion for poetry. "Writing poetry has always been my way of expressing what I can't say out loud," he said, his eyes reflecting the sincerity of his words.

Sakshi's eyes lit up with interest. "That's amazing, Kunal. I love traveling and exploring new places. It's my way of finding inspiration and understanding different cultures." Kunal smiled, fascinated. "That sounds incredible. Maybe we can share our experiences sometime. I'd love to hear about your travels, and I can share some of my poems." "I'd like that," Sakshi responded, her voice carrying a hint of excitement. "I believe there's a lot we can learn from each other." As they continued talking, Sakshi found herself increasingly intrigued by their conversation. Kunal seemed to be the most positive person she had ever met. His focus and calmness were at another level, and his words were inspiring. His mindset about the game and life in general was refreshing, and she felt drawn to his perspective.

The night wore on, and the restaurant began to empty. Despite the bustling atmosphere around them, Kunal and Sakshi remained deeply engaged in their conversation, discussing everything from their favorite foods to their dreams and aspirations. Each word seemed to weave a deeper connection between them. When it was finally time to leave, Kunal felt a sense of contentment he hadn't known in a long time. The night had brought unexpected joys, and as he walked back to the hostel under the soft glow of the streetlights, he replayed every moment of his conversation with Sakshi. Each word, each smile, etched deeper into his memory, making him look forward to the days ahead. Siddharth, walking alongside him, nudged him gently, a knowing look in his eyes. "Now do you see why I kept pushing you to talk to her? Huh? Huh? Huuhhhh?" Kunal just smiled, a soft chuckle escaping him. "Yes, yes, yesss."

Back at the girls' hostel, as the laughter and chatter from the evening's outing filled the common room, Sakshi found herself surrounded by her teammates and close friends, all bubbling with energy from the night's celebrations. However, the topic quickly shifted from basketball to something—or rather, someone—else. "So, Sakshi, someone seemed quite smitten tonight, huh?" teased Aarohi, one of her friends, as she nudged her playfully. Sakshi's cheeks flushed a light pink, and she waved her hand dismissively. "Oh, come on. We were just talking about class and basketball." "Just talking, huh? He couldn't take his eyes off you, and you two seemed pretty cozy in that corner," chimed in another friend, Priya, with a wink. The group erupted in giggles, teasing Sakshi about the obvious chemistry that seemed to spark in the dim light of the restaurant.

Trying to steer away from the spotlight, Sakshi laughed, attempting to brush off the comments. However, later that night, in the quiet of their room, she found herself opening up to Anjali, who had observed the night's proceedings with a more discerning eye. "I don't know, Anjali," Sakshi confessed, her voice a mix of confusion and excitement. "I've noticed him too, since the tryouts. There's just something about him. And tonight, talking to him felt so... easy. Like I want to do it more." Anjali smiled, sensing the depth of her friend's feelings more than Sakshi herself did. "It sounds like you're more than just a little interested, Sakshi. He seems like a great guy, and you two definitely have something. Maybe it's worth exploring?" Sakshi bit her lip, pondering. "Maybe you're right. I don't know what this is exactly, but it made me happy. Really happy."

Their conversation drifted into the night, filled with possibilities and the anticipation of what the new semester might bring. Sakshi lay in bed later, her thoughts wandering back to Kunal's smile, his gentle demeanor, and the undeniable connection that seemed to pulse between them. As sleep finally claimed her, her mind replayed their conversation, each word echoing with the promise of something new and thrilling.

ppp

7

Classes, Collaborations, and a Comforting Hug

The sunrays filtered through the vertically paneled windows of the lecture hall, casting long shadows across the rows of wooden desks. Kunal found a seat near the middle of the room, opened his notebook and got his pen out, ready to take notes. The low hum of the students talking filled the classroom, along with the occasional scrape of chairs and the thud of textbooks being set down. As Sakshi entered the room, her eyes swept across the crowded space, locking eyes with Kunal for a fleeting moment that seemed to stretch longer than it should. She smiled as she made her way towards him.

"Mind if I join you?" Sakshi asked, her voice a mix of cheerfulness and a subtle warmth that didn't escape Kunal's notice. "Of course, have a seat," Kunal replied, trying to sound casual, but his heart raced a bit faster at her proximity. As they settled into their seats, the professor—an elderly man with a reputation for his rigorous standards and engaging lectures—began the class. Today's discussion revolved around strategic business management, a subject both Kunal and Sakshi were eager to delve into. The professor announced that they would be working on a project that would last the entire semester and that thye would have to work in pairs, Kunal felt an immediate, silent hope that he and Sakshi could team up.

When the professor asked the students to pair up, Sakshi turned to Kunal, her eyes glittering with a mixture of excitement and amusement. "Looks like we're partners, then?" she suggested, and Kunal could only nod, feeling like things were falling into place perfectly. Their project discussion started with the usual exchange of ideas and thoughts about potential topics, but it quickly deepened into a more engaging dialogue about their respective visions for the project. Sakshi's insights into business dynamics were not only astute but also reflected a depth that Kunal admired. He found himself more and more impressed not just by her intelligence but by the way her mind worked, weaving theoretical knowledge with practical applications.

As the class ended and they packed up their materials, Kunal felt a sense of reluctance to part ways. Sensing a similar hesitation in Sakshi, he ventured, "Do you want to grab a coffee? Maybe we can brainstorm some more about the project and... other stuff?" Sakshi's response was immediate and enthusiastic. "I'd like that!" Their walk to the campus café was filled with a comfortable chatter. Over two steaming cups of coffee, their conversation flowed from academic topics to personal interests. Kunal shared his passion for poetry, revealing a side of him that involved more creativity and emotion than what the basketball court displayed. Sakshi, in turn, talked about her love for painting and how she found solace in art.

This first shared class and the subsequent coffee hangout marked the beginning of many. Each meeting, each project session, seemed to effortlessly weave their lives closer, a tapestry of shared interests and mutual respect forming between them. Kunal found himself looking forward to each class not just for the academic challenge but for the simple joy of Sakshi's company. And as they continued to meet, the foundation of a strong friendship was laid, one filled with laughter, banter, and an unspoken understanding that they were possibly on the brink of something more deeper than they had initially anticipated. After the eventful day, both Kunal and Sakshi were unwinding in the comfort of their respective hostels, reflecting on the newfound friendship that was blossoming with each interaction.

Kunal dropped onto his bed, the springs creaking slightly under his weight. He turned to Sid, who was watching something on his laptop and recounted the events of the day. "So, you and Sakshi, huh? That's moving along well," Siddharth teased, his voice ringing with a mix of jest and genuine curiosity. Kunal sighed, a smile tugging at his lips. "Yeah, she's...she's really something. But hey, we're just friends, Sid. We're partners for a project, and I want to keep it that way for now. See where it goes, you know?"

Siddharth chuckled. "Sure, buddy, just friends. Got it. But don't wait too long; you might miss your shot." Meanwhile, in the women's hostel, Sakshi sat cross-legged on her bed, forcing Anjali to keep her novel away and listen to her. Her voice was animated as she described how well she and Kunal had connected, not just academically but on a personal level too. Anjali's response was warm and encouraging, tinged with a hint of playfulness. "So, is this going towards something more, Sakshi? You two seem to click really well." Sakshi paused, considering. "I like him, Anjali, I do. And I feel there's something there, but I want to start with friendship. We're in no rush, right? Let's see how it goes." "Absolutely," Anjali agreed, her voice soothing. "Taking it slow sounds like a good plan. Just don't be too slow!"

Both conversations, though in two separate buildings, mirrored a similar sentiment—a desire to deepen their friendship without rushing, acknowledging a connection that both hoped would organically evolve into something more profound. Both Kunal and Sakshi expressed a serene contentment with their growing rapport, appreciating the ease and comfort they found in each other's company. This mutual feeling, though not declared openly, was evident in the way they spoke of each other—an unsaid acknowledgment of a special bond forming just steps away within the same campus. The next day, they decide to meet in the library to start working on their project. It's mid-semester at UPES, and the air in the library is thick with the scent of books and the quiet murmur of concentrated effort. Kunal and Sakshi find a quiet corner, their workspace an organized chaos of academic materials and digital tools. As they settle into their routine, the energy between them is palpable, a blend of focus and subtle excitement about what they're about to uncover together.

Their project, centered around "Innovative Business Strategies in Emerging Markets," involves analyzing case studies from different continents and industries. Sakshi proposes examining the renewable energy sector in Asia, sparked by a recent article she read on solar energy innovations in India. Kunal, intrigued, adds a comparative analysis with the tech startup ecosystems in Latin America, providing a robust framework for their project. As they delegate tasks, their strengths complement each other—Sakshi's creative insights mesh perfectly with Kunal's methodical approach to data. Each session is a deep dive into emerging markets, but it's their method of interaction that deepens their connection. They challenge each other's viewpoints, leading to spirited debates that often end with laughter and mutual respect for differing perspectives.

During coffee breaks, they share stories from their lives. Sakshi talks about her time as an NCC cadet, her eyes lighting up with enthusiasm. She describes her fascination with rifles and the thrill of extensive training sessions. "There was this one time," she begins, her voice animated, "we had a climbing exercise at a training camp. It was supposed to be a simple ascent, but halfway up, I lost my footing and fell hard. I sprained my ankle pretty badly." Kunal listens intently, his attention undivided as she continues, "I tried to fight through the pain, but it was too much. In the end, I called my parents to come and get me. They weren't too thrilled about having to drop their chores midway and come get me, but they understood! It was an intense and painful experience, but I couldn't wait to get back into training once I recovered." She smiles, reminiscing about the camaraderie and the discipline that came with being an NCC cadet. "I loved every bit of it—the early morning drills, the precision required in handling rifles, and the sheer physical endurance it demanded. Even the setbacks were part of the adventure."

As the weeks pass, their meetings become something they both look forward to. There's an ease between them that goes beyond academic partnership. They start arriving earlier to catch up on their day before diving into work, and their conversations increasingly stray towards personal ambitions and past experiences. It's during these moments that they discover shared values and a similar sense of humor, which makes their sessions not just productive but deeply enjoyable. One late evening, as they're about to conclude a particularly intense study session, Kunal notices Sakshi shivering slightly—the air conditioning in the library is too high. Without a word, he gets up and calls the admin team, asking them to increase the temperature. When he returns, Sakshi looks up, surprised and happy. She gives him a warm smile, touched by the gesture. Their eyes lock for a moment—a silent acknowledgment of the shift in their dynamics. It's brief but significant, showing the care and thoughtfulness growing in their friendship.

As they pack up to leave, there's a lingering smile on both their faces. Walking out of the library, they talk about the upcoming weekend, and without planning, they agree to meet up for a casual study session in the park. It's a small decision, but it marks a significant milestone. They are no longer just project partners; they are friends who enjoy each other's company, in and out of academic confines. As the semester progresses, the casual hangouts between Kunal and Sakshi become a cherished part of their week. These gatherings are spontaneous and varied, often including other friends but sometimes just the two of them, giving them the space to unwind and connect on a more personal level.

The university's student council frequently organizes open-air movie screenings, and these events become a regular outing for Kunal and Sakshi. Under the starry sky, they watch everything from Bollywood classics to Hollywood blockbusters. During a particularly poignant scene in a film, they share a look of mutual understanding, their reactions so in sync it surprises them both. It's moments like these, laughing over corny lines or discussing a character's motivations, that weave a deeper thread into the fabric of their growing friendship. The small café near the campus becomes their go-to spot on Wednesday nights for quiz competitions. Teaming up, they navigate through rounds of trivia questions ranging from science and history to music and sports. Sakshi's quick thinking complements Kunal's enthusisasm making them an unbeatable team. Their victories at these quiz nights are celebrated with shared desserts, their joyful competitiveness a testament to their seamless teamwork.

Sometimes, the best conversations happen during their walks around the lush, expansive campus. These walks are never planned; they start as a way to stretch their legs after a long study session but soon turn into exploratory talks where they share dreams and personal histories. Sakshi talks about her aspiration to integrate sustainable practices in business, her eyes glowing with determination and hope. Kunal listens intently, genuinely interested, and shares his own vision of one day starting a consultancy that helps small businesses thrive. On one such walk, they find themselves at the small lake near the outskirts of the campus. Sitting on a bench, they watch the sunset paint the sky in a beautiful mix of orange and pink hues. The conversation turns to their families, values, and the things that actually matter to them. As they talk, Sakshi opens up about her fears and insecurities. She shares how she often feels the weight of expectations from society and her relatives, who have always believed that girls should not be given too much freedom. This pressure sometimes leads her to overthink, worrying about what if she doesn't succeed. However, she acknowledges that she has no option but to work hard and leave the fear of failure far behind her. Kunal listens attentively, offering understanding and support. He reminds her that she doesn't need to prove anything to anyone but herself. Sakshi finds Kunal's words reassuring.

It's during these short yet personal meetups that Kunal and Sakshi slowly start to see each other not just as friends but as someone special. Someone who understands them without judgment. The ease with which they talk about their lives, the laughter they share, and the comfort they find in each other's company subtly transform their relationship, unknow even to them. They haven't spoken of it yet, but there's an unspoken understanding of the special bond forming between them. As Kunal and Sakshi's friendship deepens, the two of them walking around becomes a common sight both on and off the basketball court, leading to playful accusations from their best friends, Siddharth and Anjali. These funny complaints find their way into many of their group hangouts, adding a humorous twist to their gatherings.

During basketball practices, as the teams run drills, Siddharth starts throwing mock-accusatory glances at Kunal whenever he catches him glancing Sakshi's way. One time, after Kunal passes the ball a bit too perfectly to Sakshi, Siddharth can't resist commenting loud enough for a few nearby teammates to hear, "Hey Kunal, trying to score points on and off the court, huh?" The remark sends a ripple of laughter through some of their teammates, while Kunal just shakes his head, his face turning a shade of red, and Sakshi hides her smile behind a quick hand gesture of mock disapproval. At one of their favorite café's trivia nights, as the group huddles around a small table cluttered with snacks and quiz sheets, Anjali leans towards Sakshi, whispering just loud enough for Kunal to hear, "Sakshi, make sure Kunal doesn't just charm the answers out of you." Her comment earns an eye roll from Sakshi and chuckles from the group, including a sheepish grin from Kunal. "Hey, I'm here for the quiz, not just the charming company," Kunal retorts, which only makes the group laugh harder, including Siddharth who adds, "Yeah right, as if we'd believe that!"

During a pause in one of their practice sessions, as the players hydrate and catch their breaths, Siddharth sidles up to Kunal, slinging an arm around his shoulders. "You know, I used to be the best friend until someone started stealing all the limelight with her crossover dribbles both on the court and in your life," he jests, giving Kunal a nudge. Kunal, chuckling, tries to defend himself, "Come on, Sid, you know you'll always be my main man!" to which Siddharth theatrically wipes a fake tear, "I'm so touched, but make sure Sakshi doesn't hear that." During one of their regular girls' night out, as they all gathered around a cozy corner of their favorite café, Anjali, with a dramatic sigh, lays down a playful rule, "Okay, I'm making it official—no basketball talk tonight, and definitely no discussions about Kunal. It's like there's nothing else in the world!" The girls chuckle, nodding in mock-serious agreement. Sakshi, with a quick wit, fires back, "Agreed, and let's also put a ban on Korean TV shows, Anjali. We need a break from your K-drama spoilers!" The table bursts into laughter as Anjali feigns indignation, "Fine, but you all are missing out on the best plot twists!" This banter, full of teasing and laughter, highlights the vibrant dynamics of their friendship, making their evenings together a cherished escape from the routine.

A few days later, the friends group met up at the quaint campus café and settled around a large rustic table, the aroma of fresh coffee mingling with the chatter of students. While Siddharth animatedly recounted a recent classroom mishap, everyone laughed and sipped their drinks. However, Kunal noticed that Sakshi seemed unusually quiet, her eyes distant and her usual spark dimmed. After a moment, she excused herself from the table, stepping out into the adjoining garden, a small, serene spot with a few benches and an array of blooming flowers. Concerned, Kunal excused himself and followed her, finding her standing by a fountain, her posture tense. "Hey, Sakshi... everything okay?" Kunal approached cautiously, his voice soft. Sakshi startled slightly, then managed a weak smile. "Oh, Kunal, hi... Yeah, I'm fine, just a bit..." Her voice trailed off as she looked away, the strain evident in her eyes. Kunal stepped closer, his concern growing. "You know you can tell me if something's wrong," he urged gently.

After a hesitant pause, her defense crumbles and her voice grows softer. Her words heavy with sadness as she revisits a conversation they had a few days ago about the pressures from her relatives. "I talked to my mom earlier today," she begins, her tone tinged with distress. "She told me that one of my uncles yelled at her because I'm studying out of town and participating in sports. He believes women should stay indoors and shouldn't be exposed to the outside world so much. It was really hard to hear her so upset. My dad was there too, trying to defend our choices, and it just breaks my heart to see them going through this." Kunal listens, his face reflecting his concern. He remembers their discussions about the backward mindset some of her relatives held. "It's incredibly tough to hear that, and I'm sorry your parents are being put through this just because they support you," he says, his voice filled with empathy. Sakshi nods. "They are my pillars, Kunal. Seeing them upset because they're supporting my dreams—it's just so unfair, she confessed, her voice cracking slightly as she fought back tears. Kunal's heart ached at her words. Instinctively, he reached out, his arms hesitating in the air before he decided to pull her into a gentle hug.

Sakshi, overwhelmed by her emotions and the unexpected comfort, leaned into him, her tears finally escaping as she found solace in his embrace. It was a gentle, respectful embrace, yet charged with a tenderness that surprised them both. As he held her, Sakshi's initial stiffness melted away; she nestled closer, her breath catching as she allowed herself the vulnerability of the moment. The world seemed to hold its breath, the only sounds were the distant hum of campus life and the soft murmur of the fountain beside them. Kunal felt a warmth spread through him as Sakshi relaxed in his arms. His heart raced with a mix of concern for her pain and elation at the trust she was showing him. He could feel her breathing, slow and unsteady, and it made him want to protect her, to shield her from her sorrow. It was a hug that hinted at the deeper layers of connection that neither had fully acknowledged until now.

For a few seconds, they stood there, holding each other in the quiet garden. Kunal felt a surge of protectiveness and warmth, his heart pounding with the intensity of the moment. Sakshi, caught in her grief, momentarily forgot everything but the comforting presence of Kunal. As they slowly pulled apart, Sakshi's eyes met Kunal's, both searching for an assurance that the intimacy hadn't crossed a line. There was a brief, deafening silence where everything seemed to hang in the balance, then Sakshi whispered a heartfelt, "Thank you, Kunal. I... I needed that." Kunal, his cheeks flushed with a mix of joy and nervousness, nodded, his smile tentative. "Anytime, Sakshi. I'm here for you."

They walked back to the group together, the air between them filled with a new understanding and closeness that neither could completely define. They were reeling from the unexpected depth of connection they'd just experienced. While Sakshi was flustered by how much she had appreciated his comfort, Kunal was elated, the memory of the hug lingering like a promise.

❦❦❦

8
A Sunrise to Remember

Back at their respective hostels, both Kunal and Sakshi were unable to shake off the warmth and intimacy of their unexpected embrace. Each was deep in conversation with their closest confidant, unpacking their feelings and the implications of what had just happened.

In Kunal's Room

Kunal sat on the edge of his bed, hands clasped, his mind replaying every moment of the hug with Sakshi. The room was dim, lit only by a small desk lamp, casting long shadows that mirrored the evening's revelations. Siddharth, ever the observant friend, watched Kunal's thoughtful expression and couldn't hold back his curiosity. "Okay, out with it, man. You've been staring at that spot on the wall for an hour now. What happened with Sakshi?" Kunal sighed, a small smile playing on his lips as he met Siddharth's inquisitive gaze. "It was... different, Sid. I hugged her because she was upset, but it felt like something shifted," he confessed, his voice a mix of wonder and nervousness. "Shifted, huh? Sounds like you're falling for her, Kunal. What did she say?" Siddharth probed, leaning forward, his elbows resting on his knees. "She thanked me... and it was a simple hug, but I felt like we connected on a whole new level. It's hard to explain," Kunal tried to articulate the flood of emotions he felt, his hands gesturing in the air as if to pluck the right words from it. Siddharth chuckled, clapping him on the shoulder. "I don't need it explained, buddy. I can see it on your face. You like her a lot, don't you?" Kunal nodded, the realization dawning on him as he spoke it aloud. "Yeah, I do. And I think I want to see where this could go."

In Sakshi's Room

Sakshi sat cross-legged on her bed, her mind swirling with thoughts of the hug. Anjali, her best friend, sat beside her, a knowing smile on her face, eager to hear everything. "So, come on, Sakshi. Tell me about this hug! That's not just a friendly hug from the sound of it," Anjali nudged her gently, her eyes twinkling with excitement. Blushing, Sakshi recounted the moment. "It was comforting... and more. I didn't realize how much I needed that support until Kunal just... was there. And when he hugged me, I felt safe, you know?" Anjali watched Sakshi's expressions, noticing the deeper emotions playing across her face. "It sounds like you're feeling something strong for him. Do you think he feels the same?" Sakshi hesitated, her heart hopeful but her mind clouded with doubt. "I'm not sure. He's always so kind and considerate. Maybe he's just being a good friend?" Anjali reached out, squeezing her hand. "Maybe, but from what you've told me about how you two are together, it sounds like there might be more. Just keep an open mind, Sakshi. Sometimes, friendship is just the beginning." Both conversations, filled with encouragement and the teasing only close friends can offer, ended on a note of hopeful anticipation. Kunal and Sakshi, though unsure of the future, felt a certain clarity about their feelings. The next step seemed daunting, but with their friends' support, both felt ready to explore the depths of their connection.

The next few days were a whirlwind of anxiety and anticipation for Kunal. The hug had solidified his feelings for Sakshi, and he was determined to express them in the most memorable way possible. However, his newfound resolve also turned him into a ball of anxious mess. Every time Kunal saw Sakshi, his heart raced, and his mind scrambled for words. His usually steady hands fidgeted with anything he could find—his pen, his phone, the hem of his shirt. During their conversations, he was often distracted, his thoughts drifting to the upcoming proposal, leaving Sakshi puzzled by his sudden shiftiness. "Is everything okay, Kunal?" Sakshi asked one afternoon, her eyes searching his face for answers. They were sitting in the campus café, and Kunal had been unusually quiet, barely touching his coffee. Kunal forced a smile, avoiding her gaze. "Yeah, just a lot on my mind. You know, projects and all," he mumbled, feeling a pang of guilt for not being entirely truthful. Sakshi nodded, though her concern deepened. She couldn't shake the feeling that something had changed since their hug. Kunal seemed distant, and it stung her more than she wanted to admit. Whenever he had a spare moment, Kunal made flimsy excuses to rush off and meet Siddharth and Anjali. "I need to check on some notes with Sidd," he would say, or "Anjali and I have to finalize some details for our group project." His friends, aware of his plan, played along, but the secrecy took its toll on Sakshi.

One evening, as they walked back from the library, Sakshi's voice broke the silence. "You've been really busy lately, Kunal. It feels like we don't get to talk much anymore." Kunal's heart sank. He stopped walking and turned to face her, taking a deep breath. "I'm sorry, Sakshi. I promise it's just temporary. There's something... important I'm working on." Sakshi forced a smile, trying to hide her disappointment. "It's okay, Kunal. I understand." But she didn't, not fully. The distance hurt, and she missed the ease and warmth of their previous interactions. Little did she know, Kunal was preparing for a moment that he hoped would bring them even closer. Kunal met Siddharth and Anjali in a quiet corner of the library, their heads huddled together over a table littered with sketches, notes, and a map of the hiking trail. "I need this to be perfect," Kunal said, his voice a mix of determination and anxiety. "I want to propose to her at sunrise. It has to be special." Siddharth grinned, clapping Kunal on the back. "Relax, man. We've got this. Anjali and I have scouted the perfect spot—a quaint hut with an amazing view of the sunrise." Anjali added, "We'll decorate the place with flowers and lights. It'll be magical, trust us." Kunal nodded, his anxiety easing slightly at their confidence. "And I've written a poem.

I'll read it to her when we get there."

Over the next few days, they finalized the details. Siddharth and Anjali gathered flowers and lights, coordinating the decorations. They practiced the route to ensure everything would go smoothly. Kunal, though still a bundle of nerves, felt a growing excitement. The anticipation of the moment kept him going, despite the guilt he felt for his temporary distance from Sakshi. Finally, the day arrived. Kunal's nerves were electric as he finalized the plans with Siddharth and Anjali. The three of them had put in meticulous effort to make sure everything was perfect. When everything was set, Kunal approached Sakshi with the invitation. "Hey, Sakshi," Kunal said, trying to keep his voice casual. "How about a trek tomorrow morning? Just the two of us. I know a great spot to watch the sunrise." Sakshi, still feeling the sting of Kunal's recent aloofness, initially masked her true feelings. "I don't know, Kunal. It's pretty early, and we have a lot going on." Kunal's heart sank momentarily, but he pressed on, trying to convey his sincerity. "Please, Sakshi. I promise it'll be worth it. I... really want you to come."

After a moment of hesitation, Sakshi relented, her curiosity piqued despite her reservations. "Okay, fine. I'll go with you." The next morning, the air was crisp and fresh, carrying the scent of dew-covered grass. Kunal and Sakshi set out on their trek just as the first light of dawn began to peek over the horizon. The path was familiar, yet each step felt laden with the significance of what was to come. Kunal, despite his racing heart, tried to maintain a calm facade. He chatted easily, his usual warmth and humor slowly easing back into his tone. "Remember the last time we came this way? You almost slipped on that rock," he said, pointing out the spot with a grin. Sakshi laughed, the sound light and relieving to Kunal's anxious mind. "Yeah, and you saved me with that dramatic dive. Good times."

As they walked, their conversation flowed naturally, laughter and shared stories making the journey seem shorter. Sakshi felt a weight lift from her shoulders, relieved that Kunal was back to his old self. Little did she know, Kunal's heart was beating a mile a second. Unbeknownst to Sakshi, Siddharth and Anjali were following them from a safe distance, capturing the entire journey on camera as Kunal had requested. They made sure to stay out of sight, but their excitement mirrored Kunal's as they anticipated the big moment. When they reached the tea stall, a familiar spot for the four of them, Sakshi gasped in awe. The small hut was beautifully decorated with flowers and soft, twinkling lights. The first light of dawn painted the sky in hues of pink and orange, casting a warm glow over everything. The decorations transformed the humble tea stall into a magical setting.

"Kunal, this is amazing!" Sakshi exclaimed, her eyes shining with excitement and curiosity. Kunal took her hand, leading her to a spot where they could sit and watch the sunrise. "There's something I need to tell you," he began, his voice trembling slightly. He pulled out the folded piece of paper, his hands shaking. Sakshi's expression turned serious, her eyes never leaving Kunal's face as he began to read his poem.

These drops of rain remind me of you,
As winter reminds me of the dew,
Without any worries and full of charm,
How you too fell into my arms.

These drops are lonely and tiny in size,
But meeting earth, they unionize,
The fragrance of our love will spread everywhere,
As the earth smells fresh in the air.

Drowning into each other, we will rise,
Holding you will be prioritized,
I know, I am very wise,
But without you, my heart cries.

These drops of rain remind me of you,
There's nothing that I can't do,
Yet I am not sure if I can woo.
These drops of rain remind me of you.

As he finished, the first rays of the sun broke over the horizon, bathing them in golden light. Kunal looked up to see tears streaming down Sakshi's face. She was smiling, her emotions clear in her eyes. "Kunal... yes. Yes, I will," she whispered, her voice choked with emotion. Kunal's heart soared as he pulled her into a tight embrace, feeling the warmth of her acceptance wash over him. They stood there, holding each other, as the sun continued to rise, symbolizing the beginning of their new journey together. Hand-in-hand, they walked, their fingers intertwined. The slow rain began to fall, adding a magical touch to the morning. They talked in hushed tones, the excitement drowning their voices.

"Kunal, are you sure about this? About us?" Sakshi asked, her voice soft yet searching. Kunal stopped walking and turned to face her, his eyes filled with sincerity. "I've never been more sure of anything in my life, Sakshi. You bring out the best in me. Every moment with you feels right." Sakshi smiled, her heart swelling with love and relief. "You make me feel safe, Kunal. I've been scared, but I realize now that I want to be with you, no matter what." Kunal gently cupped her face, wiping away a stray tear with his thumb. "We'll face everything together, Sakshi. I promise."

Their conversation was interrupted by the sudden appearance of Siddharth and Anjali, who jumped out from their hiding places, unable to contain their excitement. "Surprise!" they shouted, grinning from ear to ear. Sakshi jumped back in surprise, then burst into laughter. "You two were in on this the whole time?" she asked in a mock-accusatory tone. Anjali giggled, "Guilty as charged! Kunal needed our help to make this perfect." Sakshi shook her head, still laughing. "How long has this been going on?" Siddharth answered, "A few days. Kunal here has been a nervous wreck trying to keep it a secret." Turning to Anjali, Sakshi playfully nudged her. "And you didn't tell me anything? Especially when I was upset about Kunal being so distant?" Anjali feigned innocence. "Hey, I was sworn to secrecy. Plus, it was worth it, right?" Sakshi smiled, nodding. "Yeah, it was definitely worth it."

The four friends settled down at the tea stall, the familiar and comforting smell of brewing tea wafting through the air. They sat around a small table, laughing and talking, the joy of the moment enveloping them. They replayed the scenes captured on the camera, reliving the moments. Siddharth raised his cup in a toast. "To Kunal and Sakshi. May this be just the beginning of many beautiful memories together." Anjali joined in, lifting her cup. "To love, friendship, and unforgettable moments."

Kunal and Sakshi clinked their cups with Siddharth and Anjali's, their hearts full. As they sipped their tea, the warmth of the beverage and the love shared among friends made everything feel just right. In that moment, everything felt perfect, and Kunal knew he had found his forever in Sakshi.

9

Blooming Romance and a Birthday to Remember

The days that followed Kunal's heartfelt proposal were filled with a new kind of magic. The campus seemed brighter, the air sweeter, as Kunal and Sakshi's relationship blossomed into something truly beautiful. Their friends, who had been cheering from the sidelines, now celebrated openly, thrilled to see the couple so happy together. Every day brought new moments of tenderness and love, painting their world with hues of joy and contentment. However, being in a college campus meant that open displays of affection had to be kept discreet. This added an element of excitement and secrecy to their blooming romance.

One crisp morning, as Sakshi walked across the quadrangle towards her class, Kunal spotted her from a distance. He couldn't resist the urge to surprise her, but he knew he had to be subtle. Moving quietly, he snuck up behind her and gently whispered, "Guess who?" Sakshi jumped slightly, her surprise quickly turning into a smile. "Kunal! You scared me," she whispered, glancing around to make sure no one noticed. Kunal grinned, his eyes sparkling with mischief. "Just wanted to see you smile," he said softly, resisting the urge to pull her into a hug right there.

Later that week, they found a quiet spot under a large oak tree on campus, their favorite place to steal moments together. Sakshi sat with her back against the tree, and Kunal lay down with his head in her lap. The gentle breeze rustled the leaves above them, casting dappled sunlight over their faces. Kunal closed his eyes, feeling completely at peace as Sakshi's fingers threaded through his hair. "This feels nice," he murmured, his voice soft and content. Sakshi smiled, looking down at him with a tenderness that made her heart swell. "I could stay like this forever," she whispered, enjoying the simple intimacy of the moment. Kunal opened his eyes, gazing up at her. "Me too," he said, reaching up to gently trace the outline of her face with his fingertips. "You make everything better, Sakshi."

One afternoon, they decided to take a walk outside the campus. The streets were bustling with activity, vendors calling out their wares, and the aroma of street food mingling with the fresh scent of flowers from nearby stalls. As they strolled hand-in-hand, Kunal suddenly stopped and looked around with a playful smile. "I'll be right back, wait here," he said mysteriously and darted off before Sakshi could ask where he was going. Sakshi stood there, puzzled but intrigued, as she watched Kunal disappear into the crowd. After a few minutes, he returned, his hands hidden behind his back. With a flourish, he presented her with a beautiful bouquet of lavender and white roses. "For you," he said, his eyes shining with love and excitement. Sakshi's eyes widened in surprise and delight. "Kunal, they're beautiful!" she exclaimed, taking the flowers from him and inhaling their sweet fragrance. "Not as beautiful as you," Kunal said, pulling her into a gentle hug. "I just wanted to see you smile." Sakshi's eyes shimmered with happiness as she kissed his cheek. "You always know how to make my day."

Their relationship grew stronger with each passing day, filled with moments of pure joy and affection. One sunny Saturday, Kunal and Sakshi decided to go shopping together. They wandered through the bustling streets, enjoying the lively atmosphere of the marketplace, but keeping a respectful distance when necessary to avoid unwanted attention. Sakshi stopped in front of a boutique, her eyes catching on a simple yet elegant top displayed in the window. "What do you think of that one?" she asked, glancing at Kunal. Kunal tilted his head, considering. "It's nice, but I think you'd look even better in something like this," he said, pointing to a nearby dress—a flowing, pastel-colored piece that seemed to glow in the sunlight. Sakshi's eyes lit up. "You have great taste," she said, impressed. "Let's try it on." Inside the boutique, Sakshi emerged from the dressing room wearing the dress. Kunal's breath caught in his throat as he took her in. "You look stunning," he said, his voice filled with admiration. Sakshi twirled, feeling the fabric swirl around her. "I love it. You always know what suits me best." Kunal smiled, feeling a deep sense of satisfaction. "I just know you, Sakshi. And I love seeing you happy."

As Kunal and Sakshi's relationship became more evident, their friends couldn't help but join in their joy. One evening, the group gathered at their favorite café, a cozy spot filled with the rich aroma of coffee and the sound of soft chatter. Siddharth and Anjali had been particularly eager to hear all the details. "So, how's it going, lovebirds?" Siddharth teased, nudging Kunal playfully. Kunal chuckled, his arm draped around Sakshi's shoulders. "It's going great. Better than I could have ever imagined." Anjali beamed at Sakshi. "You two are perfect together. We always knew it would happen." Sakshi blushed, feeling the warmth of their friends' support. "Thanks, guys. It means a lot to have you all with us." Siddharth raised his coffee cup in a toast. "To Kunal and Sakshi—may your love continue to grow and bring you happiness."

The group echoed the toast, their voices filled with genuine happiness for their friends. As they sipped their drinks and shared stories, the café buzzed with the vibrant energy of their camaraderie.

Their days were filled with small, sweet gestures that made each moment special. Kunal often left little notes in Sakshi's books, simple messages that made her smile. "Thinking of you," one note read, tucked into her economics textbook. Sakshi, in turn, found ways to show her affection. She would bring Kunal his favorite snacks during late-night study sessions, or send him a quick text just to say she missed him. One evening, as they sat on a bench overlooking the campus, Kunal pulled Sakshi close, wrapping his arm around her. "You know, every day with you feels like a gift," he said softly. Sakshi rested her head on his shoulder, her heart full. "And you're the best gift I could ever ask for, Kunal." As they walked hand-in-hand back to their dorms, the future seemed bright and full of promise. They knew that whatever challenges lay ahead, they would face them together, their love a beacon of hope and strength.

And so, as the days turned into weeks, Kunal and Sakshi's relationship continued to bloom, surrounded by the support and love of their friends. The journey they had embarked on was just beginning, but it was a journey they were excited to take, side by side.

Weeks passed by and soon the day of Siddharth's birthday arrived with a sense of excitement in the air. Kunal, Sakshi, and their friends from the basketball team had planned a party at a nearby restaurant known for its cozy private cabin setup. The plan was set in motion perfectly, with everyone in high spirits and ready to celebrate.

Kunal, Sakshi, and Siddharth were the first to arrive at the restaurant. They were greeted warmly by the staff and shown to their reserved cabin, a charming space adorned with soft lighting and comfortable seating. The atmosphere was intimate, perfect for the celebration ahead. Siddharth looked around the cozy cabin, a satisfied smile on his face. "This is perfect, guys. Thanks for arranging everything," he said, genuinely touched by the effort his friends had put into making his birthday special. Kunal grinned, patting Siddharth on the back. "Anything for you, buddy. Hey, where is Anjali?"

Siddharth replied, She needed to get something from the shop next door. I'll go get her and be back in a few minutes. You two hold the fort," he said with a wink before heading out. As the door closed behind Siddharth, an unexpected silence filled the cabin. Kunal and Sakshi exchanged a glance, the room suddenly feeling a bit smaller, more intimate. They settled into the plush seats, side by side, the ambiance cozy and warm. Kunal couldn't help but notice how the soft light highlighted Sakshi's features, making her look even more beautiful. His heart started to race, and he fidgeted slightly, trying to calm the nervous excitement building within him. Sakshi sensed the shift in the atmosphere too, her own heart beating faster.

For a moment, they sat quietly, their proximity filling the space with a palpable tension. Kunal shifted closer, his hand reaching out to gently take hers. "Sakshi, I... I've been wanting to tell you something," he began, his voice soft and earnest. Sakshi looked into his eyes, her breath catching. "What is it, Kunal?" she asked, her voice barely above a whisper. Kunal took a deep breath, gathering his courage. "I've been wanting to kiss you... for a long time now," he confessed, his eyes searching hers for a reaction. Sakshi felt her heart flutter, her mind racing with the same desire she had felt for weeks. "Me too," she admitted, her voice trembling slightly with anticipation.

With a slow, deliberate movement, Kunal leaned in closer, his eyes never leaving hers. The world seemed to fade away, leaving just the two of them in that moment. As their lips met, it was as if everything else ceased to exist. The kiss was soft and tentative at first, a gentle exploration of the feelings they had been holding back. The kiss deepened, and the intensity of their emotions surged. It was a connection that went beyond words, a promise of the love they shared. For a few blissful minutes, they were lost in each other, the rest of the world forgotten. Reluctantly, they pulled back, their foreheads resting against each other as they caught their breath. "Wow," Kunal murmured, his eyes sparkling with a mixture of amazement and joy. "That was... incredible."

Sakshi nodded, her cheeks flushed and her heart pounding. "It was," she agreed, a shy smile playing on her lips. The fear of being interrupted by the waiter brought them back to reality. They quickly composed themselves, settling back into their seats. But the moment they had shared lingered between them, the memory of the kiss warming their hearts. Unable to resist the pull of their newfound connection, they leaned in for another kiss. This time, it was deeper and more passionate, their desire and affection for each other overshadowing any thoughts of the outside world. They lost themselves in the kiss, letting their emotions guide them, not caring if they were seen. Just as they pulled back from the kiss, the door creaked open, and they instinctively straightened up, half-expecting to see the waiter. Instead, Siddharth walked in, followed by Anjali, both of them carrying bags and looking cheerful.

"We're back!" Siddharth announced, oblivious to the charged atmosphere he had just walked into. "Did we miss anything?" Kunal and Sakshi exchanged a quick, knowing glance before smiling at their friends. "No, nothing much. Just waiting for you guys," Kunal replied, his voice steady despite the rush of emotions still coursing through him. As they settled back into the celebration, the waiter arrived with a tray of appetizers, momentarily distracting everyone. Kunal and Sakshi couldn't help but steal glances at each other, the shared secret of their kiss adding an extra layer of excitement to the evening. The rest of the basketball team soon arrived, filling the cabin with laughter and cheerful chatter. As they all gathered around, Siddharth was the center of attention, everyone eager to wish him a happy birthday.

"To Sid, the best captain and an even better friend!" one of their teammates toasted, raising his glass. The others quickly followed suit, their glasses clinking together in a heartfelt tribute to Siddharth. Siddharth, clearly touched, stood up to address his friends. "Thank you, everyone. This means a lot to me. Here's to all of you, for making this the best birthday ever!" he declared, his smile wide and genuine. The waiter then brought out a large birthday cake, adorned with candles. Everyone gathered around as Siddharth made a wish and blew out the candles, the room erupting in cheers. The first slice of cake was ceremoniously offered to Siddharth, but it wasn't long before Kunal playfully smeared some frosting on his face, turning the celebration into a delightful mess.

Laughter echoed through the cabin as the cake fight ensued, everyone getting in on the fun. Amidst the chaos, Kunal and Sakshi managed to steal some glances, their eyes filled with the joy of the evening and the excitement of their shared secret. As the laughter died down and everyone settled back into their seats, the group continued to toast Siddharth, sharing stories and memories. Anjali, ever the life of the party, proposed another toast. "To friendships and the moments that make life unforgettable," she said, raising her glass high. "To friendships!" everyone echoed, their glasses clinking together once more.

Throughout the evening, Kunal and Sakshi found moments to be close, their hands brushing against each other under the table, their eyes meeting across the room. Each touch, each glance, was filled with a warmth that made their hearts race. After the festivities began to wind down, the group remained in high spirits, basking in the glow of the celebration. As the night wore on, the group lingered in the cozy cabin, savoring every moment of the celebration. For Kunal and Sakshi, the evening had become more than just a birthday party. It was a milestone in their relationship, a night they would remember forever.

Finally, as the party came to a close, Siddharth stood up for one last toast. "Here's to all of us, and the memories we've made tonight. Cheers!" "Cheers!" everyone echoed, raising their glasses high.

With the final toast, the friends left the restaurant, their hearts full and their spirits high. Kunal and Sakshi walked hand in hand, stealing one last kiss under the soft glow of the streetlights. It was a perfect end to a perfect evening.

10

Secret Kisses, Hidden Hugs, and an April Fool's Prank

Kunal and Sakshi had decided to meet early at the basketball court. The campus was still and silent, the early morning mist hovering just above the ground. The first light of dawn was just beginning to peek over the horizon, casting a gentle glow on the court. Kunal arrived first, dribbling the ball softly, the sound echoing in the quiet. A few minutes later, Sakshi walked in, a smile spreading across her face as she saw him.

"Couldn't sleep?" she asked, joining him in the center of the court.

Kunal grinned. "Just excited to practice with you."

They started with some light dribbling and passing drills, their movements synchronized. The court was theirs, a private sanctuary before the rest of the team arrived at 4:30. After a particularly good play, Kunal reached out, catching Sakshi's hand. "You know," he said softly, "these early mornings are quickly becoming my favorite part of the day." Sakshi smiled, stepping closer. "Mine too," she whispered.

Without another word, they moved closer, their breaths mingling in the cool morning air. Their lips met with a gentle urgency, the world outside the court fading away. Their kiss was deep and passionate, a seamless continuation of their kiss from previous night. It was an unhurried moment of pure connection. Kunal's arms wrapped around Sakshi, pulling her closer. Sakshi's hands slid up Kunal's chest, resting on his shoulders as she leaned into the kiss. It deepened, their breaths becoming one, a silent exchange of emotions that words could never capture.

The early morning light painted a soft glow around them, the cool air amplifying the warmth between them. Kunal's fingers traced gentle patterns on Sakshi's back, pulling her even closer. She responded by threading her fingers through his hair, the kiss growing more intense, filled with a passion they had both been holding back. For a few moments, time stood still. It was just the two of them, lost in their own world. When they finally pulled apart, they stayed close, foreheads touching, breathing in sync, their eyes reflecting the shared intensity of the moment.

"We should probably get back to practice before the others arrive," Sakshi murmured, though she made no move to step away. Kunal nodded, a small smile playing on his lips. "Yeah, we should." One last quick kiss and they resumed their drills.

As their early morning practices became routine, Kunal and Sakshi's relationship grew stronger with each passing day. Between classes, Kunal and Sakshi sought out hidden corners of the campus where they could steal a few moments together. The university grounds were full of nooks and crannies that provided the perfect hideaways for their secret hugs. Behind the tall, ivy-covered walls of the old library, they found one such spot. Kunal would pull Sakshi into his arms, holding her close, feeling the steady beat of her heart against his chest. "I can't wait for our next practice," he whispered, his lips brushing her ear. Sakshi smiled, her arms wrapped tightly around him, savoring the warmth of his embrace. These brief moments provided a respite from the busy day, a chance to reconnect amidst their hectic schedules.

In another instance, they found a secluded bench behind the engineering building, shielded by large trees. Kunal sat down first, pulling Sakshi onto the bench beside him, their faces inches apart. "How's your day going?" he asked, his eyes searching hers. "Better now," she replied, leaning in close. Their heads rested against each other, sharing the quiet intimacy. These secret interludes, though fleeting, became the highlights of their day.

Their love for basketball was always visible anytime they stepped into the court together. Their synergy was undeniable. They moved in harmony, understanding each other's cues without needing to speak. They played one-on-one games, their competitive spirits driving them to improve. Their laughter and playful banter filled the court, creating an atmosphere of joy and camaraderie. One evening, as they practiced alone in the dimly lit gym, Kunal challenged Sakshi to a game. "First to ten points," he declared, a mischievous glint in his eyes.

"You're on," Sakshi replied, matching his enthusiasm.

The game was intense, filled with swift moves and sharp turns. They pushed each other to their limits, their skills evenly matched. Kunal's focus was unwavering as he dribbled the ball, his eyes locked on the hoop. But just as he was about to shoot, Sakshi stole the ball, sprinting down the court with a triumphant laugh. "Not so fast," Kunal called, chasing after her. He caught up, blocking her path, their bodies colliding gently. For a moment, they stood there, panting and grinning at each other.

"You're getting better," Kunal admitted, his voice filled with admiration.

"So are you," Sakshi replied, her eyes sparkling with excitement.

They resumed the game, each point hard-fought. When Sakshi finally scored the winning basket, Kunal laughed, pulling her into a celebratory hug. "You win this time," he conceded, his arms still around her. Their post-practice cool-downs were just as special. They sat side by side on the court, their backs against the wall, sharing a water bottle and talking about everything and nothing. The quiet moments after the intense practice sessions were where they truly connected, their conversations deepening their understanding of each other.

One evening, as they sat on the court, the gym lights casting long shadows, Sakshi leaned her head on Kunal's shoulder. "I never imagined I'd find this kind of connection here," she confessed softly. "Neither did I," Kunal replied, his hand gently stroking her hair. He remembered how she used to have short hair earlier. But on learning that he wanted to see her with long hair, she had decided to grow it out more. And Kunal never missed the opportunity to compliment her for her hair which had grown longer. One weekend, they decided to explore the city together. They started their day at a quaint local café, tucked away in a quiet corner of the bustling city. The café was known for its artisanal coffee and cozy atmosphere, making it the perfect spot for a leisurely morning.

Kunal and Sakshi sat by the window, watching the world go by as they sipped their coffee. "I love this place," Sakshi said, her eyes bright with excitement. "It's so peaceful." Kunal smiled, reaching across the table to take her hand. "I'm glad you like it." They spent the morning talking and laughing, sharing stories from their past and dreams for the future. After finishing their coffee, they wandered through the nearby markets, browsing through stalls filled with colorful trinkets and handmade crafts. They sampled street food, enjoying the rich flavors and vibrant atmosphere of the market.

As the sun began to set, Kunal and Sakshi made their way to a nearby lake. The water shimmered under the fading light, creating a serene and picturesque setting. They found a quiet spot by the shore and sat down, their shoulders touching. "This has been an amazing day," Sakshi said softly, resting her head on Kunal's shoulder. Kunal wrapped his arm around her, pulling her closer. "It has. I love spending time with you." They sat in comfortable silence, watching the sun dip below the horizon. The conversation turned to their dreams and aspirations, each of them sharing their hopes for the future.

"I want to travel the world," Sakshi said, her eyes distant as she imagined the possibilities. "There are so many places I want to see and experiences I want to have. My relatives have been holding me back all my life. But now I have decided to break free. I want to fly and explore and always have you with me." Kunal nodded, his gaze fixed on the water. "I want to be part of your future. I want you in my life. You are my future, Sakshi." Sakshi smiled, her heart swelling with affection. "I want that too."

On the rare occasions when their busy schedules prevented them from seeing each other, Kunal and Sakshi would talk over calls at night. Their conversations ranged from the mundane to the profound, each one bringing them closer together. "How was your day?" Kunal asked one evening, his voice warm and comforting. "It was good," Sakshi replied, her voice soft and content. "I had a great practice session, and I managed to finish my project."

Kunal chuckled. "You always manage to get things done! You're amazing, you know that?" Sakshi blushed, even though he couldn't see it. "Thank you. How was your day?" "It was busy, but I kept thinking about our plans for the weekend. I can't wait to see you again." These nightly calls became a way for them to unwind and feel connected, even when they were apart. One night, as they talked about their favorite books, Kunal shared a poem he had written. His voice was soft and melodic, the words flowing seamlessly.

"That was beautiful," Sakshi whispered, feeling a deep connection to his words.

"I'm glad you liked it," Kunal replied. "I wrote it for you."

Months passed by blissfully. The early April sun bathed the university campus in a warm glow. Students bustled about, eager to embrace the promise of spring. Unknown to Kunal, Sakshi had been planning a playful April Fool's prank to test his reaction and perhaps have a bit of fun.

Sakshi called Kunal in the early afternoon, asking him to meet her at their favorite café. The café was a cozy spot, tucked away from the main campus, where they often spent time together. Kunal, sensing a hint of urgency in her voice, agreed immediately and rushed over. As Kunal entered the café, he saw Sakshi sitting by the window, her expression a mix of nervousness and determination. He felt a knot form in his stomach, worried about what she had to say. "Hey, Sakshi. What's going on?" he asked, sliding into the seat across from her. Sakshi took a deep breath, looking down at her hands. "Kunal, I need to tell you something. My ex-boyfriend has been reaching out to me, and... I've been considering talking to him and... I don't know..."

Kunal's heart sank. He tried to mask his feelings with a supportive smile, but the hurt was evident in his eyes. "I understand that you had a life before we met," he said softly. "If you feel like you need to talk to him, then you should do what feels right for you." Sakshi bit her lip, watching the conflicting emotions play out on his face. She felt a pang of guilt, not expecting this reaction from him. But she pressed on. "I'm really confused, Kunal. I don't know what to do." Kunal's voice trembled slightly as he spoke. "Your happiness is more important to me than anything else. If talking to him will help you find clarity, then I support your decision." Feeling overwhelmed, Kunal stood up abruptly. "I'll see you later, Sakshi."

He walked out of the café, his mind in turmoil. Sakshi watched him go, her heart aching with regret. She quickly decided to follow him, keeping a safe distance. Kunal made his way to a nearby park, a place where they often went to relax and talk. He found a secluded bench and sat down, his shoulders slumped. Tears welled up in his eyes as he thought about the possibility of losing Sakshi. Sakshi watched from a distance, her heart breaking at the sight of Kunal's tears. She couldn't bear to see him in pain any longer. She approached him quietly, her footsteps soft on the grass.

"Kunal," she called gently. He looked up, surprised to see her standing there. "Sakshi, what are you doing here?" She took a deep breath, her voice filled with remorse. "I'm so sorry, Kunal. I was just trying to play an April Fool's prank on you. I didn't mean to hurt you." Kunal stared at her, confusion and relief washing over him. "A prank? You were joking about your ex?" Sakshi nodded, tears forming in her own eyes. "Yes, and I realize now it was a terrible idea. I'm so sorry. I never wanted to see you like this."

Kunal let out a shaky breath, wiping away his tears. "Why did you agree to it then?" Sakshi asked softly. "Why didn't you fight for us?" Kunal looked into her eyes, his voice earnest and full of love. "Because your happiness is more important to me than anything else. If talking to him would have made you happy, I would have supported you, even if it meant losing you." Sakshi felt her heart swell with emotion. She realized how deeply Kunal loved her, how selfless he was. Tears streamed down her face as she closed the distance between them, wrapping her arms around him in a tight hug. "I'm so sorry, Kunal. I love you so much, and I never want to lose you," she whispered against his shoulder.

Kunal hugged her back, his own tears flowing freely. "I love you too, Sakshi. I just want you to be happy." They held each other for a long time, the park around them fading away as they focused on the strength of their connection. The prank had revealed the depth of their feelings for each other, and as they pulled back to look into each other's eyes, they both knew their bond was unbreakable. "Let's promise to always be honest with each other," Sakshi said, her voice trembling slightly.

Kunal nodded, a small smile breaking through his tears. "I promise."

ᏡᏡᏡ

11

Fading Connections

Months had flown by, and the festive cheer had given way to a more somber atmosphere on campus. The corridors were filled with a different kind of intensity—one fueled by the pressures of assignments, group projects, and the looming shadow of final exams. These weren't just tests; they were gateways to future opportunities, and for many, like Sakshi, they were the first step towards a life of independence.

For Sakshi, the stakes were exceptionally high. These exams represented not just the culmination of her academic efforts but a chance to break free from the stifling expectations of her relatives. Every day, her routine became more regimented—back-to-back classes, endless assignments, and group study sessions that stretched late into the night. Her desk was a testament to her relentless drive, cluttered with textbooks, notes, and empty coffee cups. The dark circles under her eyes and her rarely seen dorm room spoke volumes about the sleepless nights fueled by caffeine and sheer determination.

This single-minded focus had transformed Sakshi's daily life into a continuous cycle of study and minimal rest. She often skipped meals, choosing instead to spend every spare moment revising or preparing for the next onslaught of academic challenges. Conversations with friends had become brief exchanges about study tips or exam schedules, leaving little room for casual chats, let alone anything that could lead to distraction.

But as the final exams approached, Sakshi and Kunal found themselves slipping into old habits, their frequent calls during study hours leading to unintended consequences. During the model exams, a preliminary round meant to prepare them for finals, their results were underwhelming. Sakshi, usually a high achiever, was particularly affected, her scores far below her usual standard. The disappointment hit hard, and frustration simmered as Sakshi reflected on the causes of their academic slip. The realization that their casual conversations were a significant distraction became unavoidable. With a sense of urgency, she reached out to Kunal, her tone a mix of disappointment and resolve.

"Kunal, we messed up," Sakshi began, her voice tight with frustration as they met briefly between classes. "Our scores this time? That's on us. We can't let this happen for finals."

Kunal, taken aback by the seriousness of her tone, tried to offer some reassurance, but Sakshi was quick to outline her plan. "Listen, I've been thinking about this a lot. We need a strict schedule. No more random calls or long breaks. Only urgent or study-related communications. I can't—we can't—afford to be each other's weakness, not now." Her words, though harsh, were driven by a desperate need to regain control over her academic trajectory. Kunal felt a jolt of reality; Sakshi's disappointment was a mirror to his own shortcomings.

"Are we really that bad for each other's focus?" Kunal asked, the weight of the situation settling in. "It's not about us being bad for each other," Sakshi replied quickly, her voice softening slightly with the realization of how her words might have sounded. "It's about the timing. We need to prioritize, Kunal. Our future depends on it." In the quiet of his dorm room, Kunal sat staring at his phone, the screen dark except for the schedule Sakshi had sent him. The list of rules—no calls unless urgent or study-related—felt more like a barrier than a plan. He understood the necessity, the absolute need for focus that Sakshi had emphasized, but his heart sank with the realization of what this meant for their daily interactions.

For months, Sakshi's voice had been a constant in his daily routine, a comforting presence that broke the monotony of his studies. Now, the silence felt oppressive, a stark reminder of the space growing between them. Kunal missed the easy conversations, the laughter, and the shared moments of respite from their demanding academic lives. As he lay back on his bed, Kunal tried to convince himself that this was for the best. He replayed Sakshi's words in his mind, each one echoing with a mixture of resolve and regret. He couldn't shake the feeling of sadness that washed over him each time he glanced at his phone, knowing it wouldn't light up with her casual messages or impromptu calls to take a break together.

That evening, as he walked the familiar paths they once strolled together, Kunal felt the weight of isolation more acutely. The campus, alive with the chatter of other students, seemed to mock his solitude. He realized how much he had relied on those small, stolen moments with Sakshi to keep the stress at bay. Now, each step felt heavier, each day longer. Kunal tried to focus on his studies, to fill the gaps with more coursework and extra sessions in the library. But the solitude wasn't just physical; it was emotional. The schedule wasn't just a series of time slots devoted to studying—it was a wall he wasn't sure how to scale without losing a part of what made his days bearable.

Driven by a mixture of loneliness and the stress of a demanding study load, Kunal reached out to Sakshi one evening, hoping for even a brief respite from the solitude. He dialed her number, each ring amplifying his anticipation and anxiety. On the other end, Sakshi, deeply immersed in her preparations, saw her phone light up with Kunal's name. Her initial reaction was frustration—she had been navigating through a complex problem set, and interruptions were the last thing she needed. Yet, as the phone continued to ring, her resolve wavered. Despite the strict rules they had set, the emotional pull was undeniable. With a reluctant sigh, she answered.

"Hey, Sakshi, just needed a quick break. Thought we could chat for a few minutes," Kunal's voice came through, tinged with an unmistakable note of hope. Sakshi paused, the familiarity of his voice stirring a mix of emotions. "Kunal, we agreed on no calls. You know how important this is," she reminded him gently, yet firmly. "I know, I know. I just... I miss this. Can't we just talk for a few minutes?" Kunal's plea was heartfelt, his desire for connection palpable.

They slipped into conversation, finding comfort in the familiarity and ease of their exchange. Laughter and light-hearted teasing momentarily dissolved the pressures of their academic burdens. However, as the call ended, Sakshi was left with a sinking feeling of guilt. The joy of their interaction was overshadowed by a nagging sense of failure to adhere to their agreed-upon boundaries. This pattern repeated over the next few days—Kunal initiating contact, and Sakshi, despite her initial resistance, eventually giving in. Each conversation, though filled with laughter and a temporary escape from stress, left Sakshi increasingly conflicted. The guilt of indulging in these distractions weighed heavily on her, tainting the relief they otherwise brought.

Their interactions, typically a source of strength, began to breed tension. Minor disagreements quickly escalated into arguments, each fueled by the underlying stress of their looming exams and the guilt from their repeated lapses in discipline. "Kunal, we can't keep doing this," Sakshi expressed during one of their more heated exchanges. Her voice was laden with frustration, a clear indication of her inner turmoil. "Every time we talk, it feels great, but then I'm left feeling guilty. We promised we'd focus, and it seems like we keep breaking that promise."

Kunal felt a surge of defensiveness but also understood her point. "I'm just trying to keep us connected," he responded, his voice reflecting his own struggle. "I thought we could handle a few minutes here and there." "It's not just a few minutes, Kunal, and you know it," Sakshi countered sharply. "It's about the fact that we don't stick to our plan. We agreed to limit distractions, especially now. We're risking our futures here." One afternoon, after yet another disruptive call, Sakshi's patience snapped. "Kunal, this has to stop,"

Sakshi said, her voice firm and her frustration evident. "We set these boundaries for a reason. You keep crossing them, and it's not just affecting our studies—it's affecting us."

Kunal, feeling defensive yet guilty, responded, "I know, I just..."

Realizing that their repeated failures to adhere to their plan were leading them down an unsustainable path, Sakshi decided that a more drastic measure was necessary. She asked Kunal to meet her at the park immediately and disconnected the call. The urgency and tone of the message set Kunal's nerves on edge as he made his way to the park. The path, once a symbol of their togetherness, now felt like a prelude to something foreboding. When he arrived, he saw Sakshi pacing back and forth near their usual bench, her face set in a stern expression. It was the same bench where they had spent countless evenings talking about their future, dreaming together about the lives they wanted to build. The memory of those happier times made the current tension even more painful. "What's going on, Sakshi?" Kunal asked, concern lacing his voice as he approached her.

Sakshi stopped pacing and faced him, her eyes flashing with frustration and anger. She took a deep breath, trying to steady her racing thoughts. How could she explain the pressure she felt, the constant tug-of-war between her ambitions and her feelings for Kunal? She loved him, but right now, her future depended on these exams. "Kunal, why do you keep calling me to come out for coffee or walks or just for hanging out? Why do you keep calling me during hours that are strictly allotted for studies? We need to focus on our exams right now. This isn't the time for distractions." Taken aback, Kunal tried to explain. "I'm studying, Sakshi. But I miss spending time with you. Can't we balance both?" She cut him off sharply, her voice rising. "This isn't a movie where the hero and heroine get to be romantic every second. Think practically!

We have to ace these exams and get good placements. If we ever want a future together, we need to be in strong positions career-wise. My parents won't even consider us if you don't have a stable job." Kunal felt a surge of anger and sadness but kept his voice calm, though his hands trembled slightly. "I understand, Sakshi, but I just wanted to spend a little time together and talk to you now and then. It feels like you don't miss me as much as I miss you." Sakshi was quiet momentarily, but then she hardened her stance again, crossing her arms. "I'm sorry for yelling, but nothing will change my priorities right now. These exams are everything to me. I can't afford any distractions." She hated how harsh she sounded, but she couldn't let herself get distracted, not now. Every minute spent away from her books felt like a step back from the freedom she desperately sought. The wind picked up, swirling leaves around their feet as Kunal looked at her, his heart heavy with a mix of emotions. He thought about the first time they had met here, the way her smile had lit up the entire park.

Those moments felt distant now, overshadowed by the relentless demands of their academic lives. "Okay, I get it. Do you want to grab a coffee, at least?" At that, Sakshi lost her temper again, her frustration boiling over. Her voice broke as she yelled, "Did you even listen to what I just said?" Her hands clenched into fists at her sides, her whole body trembling with the effort to hold back tears. Kunal's fists clenched in frustration, his knuckles turning white. He took a deep breath, trying to stay calm. "Sakshi, I just want us to find some time for each other. I miss you. Is that too much to ask?" Sakshi shook her head, her eyes filled with tears. "You just don't understand, Kunal. This conversation has been a waste of time." She turned and walked off, unable to hold back her tears. Kunal stood there, the chill of the wind cutting through his jacket, watching her retreating figure.

He felt a profound sense of helplessness and anger, mixed with deep sadness. The park, which had once been a place of warmth and shared moments, now felt cold and desolate. He began the walk back to his hostel room, the path seemed longer and colder than ever before. The rustling leaves and distant sounds of the campus did little to soothe his troubled mind. Once inside his room, he pulled out his phone and tried texting Sakshi: Can we please talk? There was no response. He tried calling, but it went straight to voicemail. Frustrated, he tried again, only to be met with the same silence. Feeling desperate, Kunal called Anjali. She picked up after a few rings. "Hey, Kunal. What's up?" "Anjali, have you seen Sakshi? She's not responding to my calls or texts." There was a pause on the other end before Anjali replied, "Kunal, she's really upset right now. She's not in the mood to talk. Give her some space, okay?" Kunal sighed, rubbing his temples.

"Alright, thanks, Anjali." Sakshi heard Anjali talk to Kunal, her mind racing. She was extremely upset about the conversation she'd had with him, but she knew she had to stay firm. The emotional turmoil was taking its toll, and she couldn't afford any distractions. She talked to Anjali, explaining her situation and her decision. "I just feel like we're both suffering because of this," Sakshi said, her voice shaky. "I need to focus on my studies, and he needs to understand that. It's not that I don't care about him, but right now, this is what's important." Anjali nodded sympathetically. "It's a tough decision, but if you think it's the best thing for both of you, then you should do it." Sakshi took a deep breath and picked up her phone. With a heavy heart, she typed out a message to Kunal: Kunal, I think we need to take a break until the exams and placements are done. This emotional turmoil is taking a toll on both of us. Let's focus on our priorities for now. I hope you understand.

Kunal was sitting on his bed when the message came through. He stared at the screen, his heart sinking. The words blurred as his eyes filled with tears. He read the message again, feeling a numbness spread through his body. He sank back into his bed, staring at the ceiling, unable to process the pain. Siddharth, who had just entered the room, saw Kunal's expression and walked over. "Hey, man, what's wrong?" Kunal handed him the phone without a word. Siddharth read the message and sighed, sitting down beside him. "Oh no..." Kunal closed his eyes, feeling the weight of Sakshi's decision pressing down on him like a huge boulder.

ৡৡৡ

12
Together

The days following Sakshi's message were a blur for Kunal. He retreated into a shell, barely talking to anyone. His usual confidence seemed to evaporate, replaced by a heavy silence that hung around him like a cloud. Siddharth watched his friend with growing concern, unsure how to reach out without making things worse. "Kunal, you want to grab some lunch?" Siddharth asked one afternoon, trying to sound casual. Kunal shook his head, not looking up from his books. "Not hungry, man. You go ahead."

Siddharth exchanged a worried glance with Anjali, who had been standing nearby. "This isn't good," Anjali whispered. "He's shutting everyone out." They decided to talk to Sakshi, hoping she might be able to help. They found her in the library, surrounded by stacks of textbooks and notes. "Sakshi, we need to talk," Anjali said gently. "Kunal's not doing well. He's barely eating, hardly speaking to anyone." Sakshi's face fell, a flicker of pain crossing her eyes. "I know," she said softly. "I want to talk to him, but I'm afraid that if I do, I won't be able to stop. I'll lose focus, and everything we've worked for will fall apart."

Siddharth nodded, understanding her dilemma. "He respects your decision, Sakshi. But please, just make sure he's okay. He's not handling this well." Sakshi looked down at her books, her resolve wavering. "I'll try. But please, keep an eye on him for me. I can't bear to think of him like this." As the days turned into weeks, the atmosphere on campus grew increasingly tense. Exams loomed large, and the pressure was palpable. Students crammed last-minute information in the hallways, their faces etched with worry and exhaustion.

Kunal and Sakshi ran into each other occasionally on campus, their encounters brief and awkward. They maintained a polite distance, even when their friends sat together in the cafeteria. Kunal respected Sakshi enough to honor her decision, though it was killing him inside. Sakshi, too, found it excruciatingly hard to stick to her decision, longing for the comfort of Kunal's presence. The exams began, a whirlwind of stress and anxiety. Some exams felt brutally tough, pushing students to their limits, while others seemed relatively straightforward. The night before each exam, the library was packed with students frantically revising, their eyes red from lack of sleep and caffeine consumption.

In the midst of this chaos, Kunal and Sakshi occasionally caught glimpses of each other. Kunal saw Sakshi from across the library, her head buried in a book, and his heart ached. He remembered the times they used to study together, the way she would smile at him over her notes, and how they would take breaks to talk about anything and everything. Sakshi, on the other hand, would see Kunal in the cafeteria, sitting with Siddharth and Anjali but looking distant. Her resolve would waver, and she had to fight the urge to go to him, to tell him that she missed him terribly. But she stayed firm, knowing that this was necessary for both of them to succeed.

During one particularly grueling exam, Kunal found himself struggling to concentrate. The questions seemed to blur together, his mind drifting back to Sakshi. He took a deep breath, trying to focus, but the pain of their separation was a constant distraction. After the exam, Kunal walked out of the hall, feeling defeated. He saw Sakshi standing with a group of friends, her expression a mix of exhaustion and determination. Their eyes met for a brief moment, and Kunal saw a flicker of longing in her gaze before she turned away.

In the hallways, students crammed last-minute notes, whispering formulas and theories under their breath. The air was thick with tension, and even the most prepared students felt the weight of the exams bearing down on them. As the days passed, the strain of the exams began to take its toll on everyone. Anjali and Siddharth tried their best to support both Kunal and Sakshi, but it was clear that the break was affecting them deeply. One evening, after another long study session, Siddharth found Kunal sitting alone in their dorm room, staring blankly at his notes. "Hey, you okay?" he asked, sitting down beside him.

Kunal replied with a non-committal shrug, "Yes. It's fine, Sidd." He couldn't bring himself to open up to Sidd about what he actually felt. Meanwhile, in her room, Sakshi was confiding in Anjali. "I hate this," she admitted, tears welling up in her eyes. "I hate that we're apart, but I know it's the right thing to do. We need to focus on our futures." Anjali hugged her friend tightly. "It's hard, but you're doing the right thing. Just a little longer, and then you can talk to him. You'll both be stronger for it."

As the final exams approached, the tension reached its peak. Kunal and Sakshi continued to run into each other, their encounters brief and filled with unspoken words. The campus was a hive of activity, with students frantically preparing for the last push. On the day of the last exam, Kunal arrived early, hoping to gather his thoughts. He saw Sakshi across the hall, surrounded by her friends, and their eyes met for a fleeting moment. There was a mutual understanding in their gazes, a silent promise that they would get through this. The exam was tough, but Kunal pushed through, determined to finish strong. When it was finally over, he walked out of the hall, feeling a mix of relief and exhaustion. He saw Sakshi standing by the entrance, looking just as worn out.

They approached each other slowly, the distance between them feeling both immense and insignificant. "We did it," Kunal said softly, his voice filled with emotion. Sakshi nodded, her eyes glistening with unshed tears. "Yeah, we did." For a moment, they stood there in silence, the weight of the past few weeks hanging heavy in the air. Then, without a word, they turned and walked away, each heading in different directions. The break had taken its toll, but they had survived the exams. Now, they would have to figure out how to bridge the gap that had formed between them.

Relief washed over the campus as students celebrated the end of their academic trials. Laughter and chatter filled the air, but for Kunal and Sakshi, a sense of uncertainty lingered. Kunal felt a strange emptiness. The focus that had driven him through the exams was gone, replaced by a void he couldn't quite fill. He wandered around campus, watching groups of friends laughing and planning their celebrations. He envied their carefree joy, wishing he could feel the same. Siddharth found him sitting alone on a bench near the library, staring off into the distance. "Hey, man, it's over. We should be celebrating," Siddharth said, trying to lift Kunal's spirits.

Kunal managed a weak smile. "Yeah, I know. It's just... I don't know. I feel kind of lost." Siddharth sat down beside him. "I get it. The exams were hard, but you made it through. Now it's time to figure out what comes next." Kunal nodded, but his thoughts were elsewhere. He wondered what Sakshi was doing, how she was feeling. The distance between them felt even more pronounced now that the exams were over. He pulled out his phone, scrolling through old messages from her, feeling a pang of longing.

Meanwhile, Sakshi was experiencing her own turmoil. She had thrown herself into her studies, using them as a shield against her emotions. Now that the exams were over, the full weight of her feelings came crashing down. She sat in her room, surrounded by textbooks and notes that no longer served a purpose. Anjali knocked on her door and poked her head in. "Hey, you okay? You've been in here for hours." Sakshi looked up, her eyes tired. "Yeah, I'm fine. Just... processing everything."

Anjali walked in and sat on the edge of the bed. "I know it's been tough. But you did it. The exams are over, and you should be proud of yourself." "I am proud," Sakshi said softly. "But now I have to face everything I've been pushing away." Anjali squeezed her hand. "Take it one step at a time. Maybe you should talk to Kunal. He's been going through a lot too." Sakshi's heart ached at the mention of his name. She wanted nothing more than to run to him, to apologize and make things right. "I will. I just need to sort out my own head first."

The campus buzzed with the excitement of post-exam freedom, but for Kunal and Sakshi, the future felt uncertain. They both knew they had to confront their feelings and decide what their next steps would be, not just academically but personally as well. As the sun set on the first day of their newfound freedom, Kunal walked aimlessly, finding himself at the park where he and Sakshi used to meet. The memories of their happier times together flooded back, and he felt a renewed determination. He needed to talk to her, to find out if they could bridge the gap that had formed between them.

Meanwhile, Sakshi sat by her window, watching the colors of the sunset blend into the night sky. She knew the conversation with Kunal was inevitable, and the thought both terrified and comforted her. After a few days of this uneasy truce, Kunal decided he couldn't wait any longer. He needed to talk to Sakshi, to lay everything out in the open and figure out where they stood. He sent her a message: Can we talk? I think it's time. Sakshi's heart raced when she saw the message. She had been dreading this moment, but she knew Kunal was right. They needed to talk. She replied: Yes. Meet me at the park at 5?

The familiar park had always been their place of solace, and it seemed fitting that they would meet there for this conversation. As the sun dipped below the horizon, casting long shadows over the park, Kunal arrived first, his heart heavy with anticipation. He paced nervously, rehearsing what he wanted to say, but everything felt inadequate. Sakshi arrived a few minutes later, her expression a mix of determination and apprehension. They greeted each other with a tentative smile, and for a moment, the air between them was thick with unspoken words. "Thanks for meeting me," Kunal began, his voice soft. "I've been thinking a lot about us, and I know we need to talk." Sakshi nodded, her eyes reflecting the same mix of emotions. "I've been thinking too. We can't keep going on like this."

Kunal took a deep breath, trying to steady his nerves. "I miss you, Sakshi. I miss us. But I also understand why we needed this break. The exams were difficult, and I know how important they were for both of us." Sakshi looked down, her voice trembling slightly. "I miss you too, Kunal. More than you can imagine. But I felt like I had to choose between my future and our relationship, and that was tearing me apart." Kunal stepped closer, his eyes searching hers for answers. "But it doesn't have to be one or the other, does it? Can't we find a way to support each other, to be there for each other without losing sight of our goals?"

Tears welled up in Sakshi's eyes, and she quickly wiped them away. "I want to believe that. But the pressure was so intense, and I felt like I was drowning. I didn't know how to balance everything." Kunal's voice softened, filled with vulnerability. "I was struggling too, Sakshi. I didn't handle things well, and I'm sorry for that. But I love you, and I don't want to lose what we have. I'm willing to do whatever it takes to make this work." Sakshi looked at him, her heart breaking and healing at the same time. "I love you too, Kunal. And I don't want to lose you either. But we need to figure out how to communicate better, how to support each other without losing ourselves."

Kunal nodded, his eyes shining with hope. "I agree. We need to be honest with each other, even when it's hard. And we need to make time for us, no matter how busy things get." Sakshi took his hand, squeezing it tightly. "We can do this, Kunal. We've come this far, and we can find a way forward together." They stood there for a moment, holding each other's gaze, feeling the weight of their words and the promise of a renewed commitment. The air around them felt lighter, filled with the possibility of a new beginning. Kunal pulled her into a gentle embrace, feeling the warmth of her body against his. "I've missed this," he said. "Me too... me too," Sakshi replied. "We'll take it one day at a time," he whispered. "But we'll do it together."

Sakshi nodded, her heart swelling with a mixture of relief and love. "Together."

❧❧❧

91

13
Back Together, Yet Miles Away

Things were slowly getting better between Kunal and Sakshi. After their heartfelt conversation, they both made a conscious effort to communicate better and support each other. The heavy cloud that had hung over them seemed to lift, and their friends, Siddharth and Anjali, were relieved to see them back together. However, the next hurdle came in the form of campus placements. Training sessions for placements began almost immediately after exams, and the preparation process was intense. Workshops, mock interviews, and resume building sessions filled their days, making their schedules even more hectic.

Despite the demanding schedule, Kunal and Sakshi found ways to stay connected. They would meet for quick coffee breaks between sessions or send encouraging messages throughout the day. They were determined not to let the pressures of placements drive them apart like the exams had. One evening, after a particularly grueling mock interview session, Kunal and Siddharth sat in the cafeteria, discussing their experiences. "How did your session go?" Siddharth asked, taking a sip of his coffee.

Kunal sighed, running a hand through his hair. "It was tough. The interviewer grilled me on technical questions, and I stumbled a bit. But I think I recovered okay." Siddharth nodded. "Yeah, these sessions are brutal. But they're preparing us for the real thing. How's Sakshi holding up?" Kunal smiled, his expression softening. "She's stressed, but she's handling it well. We've been making sure to talk whenever we can. It helps keep us grounded." Siddharth grinned. "I'm glad to hear that. You guys seem a lot better." Kunal nodded. "We are. It's still tough, but we're making it work."

Meanwhile, Sakshi and Anjali were in the library, going over potential interview questions and practicing their responses. "How are things with you and Kunal?" Anjali asked, glancing up from her notes. Sakshi smiled, a look of contentment on her face. "Better. We're talking more, and it feels good to be on the same page again. The placement prep is crazy, but we're managing." Anjali nodded. "I'm really happy for you two. You've been through a lot, but it seems like you're stronger for it." Sakshi sighed, flipping through her notes. "Yeah, we are. I just hope we can keep it up. These placements are no joke."

As the placement process progressed, the pressure intensified. The campus buzzed with a mix of excitement and anxiety. Students could be seen huddled in groups, practicing interview questions, or frantically updating their resumes. Kunal and Sakshi continued to support each other, sharing their fears and hopes about the future. They would meet in the evenings, often exhausted but grateful for the time together. They talked about their interviews, their worries, and their dreams, finding solace in each other's presence. Siddharth and Anjali watched their friends with a sense of pride and relief. They had seen Kunal and Sakshi at their lowest, and it was heartening to see them navigate this new challenge together.

One night, after a particularly intense day of interview prep, Kunal and Sakshi sat on a bench in the park, the same place where they had reconciled weeks before. The air was cool, and the stars twinkled above them. "I'm so tired," Sakshi admitted, leaning her head on Kunal's shoulder. "But I'm glad we have this time together." Kunal wrapped his arm around her, pulling her close. "Me too. We'll get through this, just like we did the exams." Sakshi nodded, feeling a sense of peace. "Together."

Finally, the first of many days of the placement process arrived. The campus was buzzing with a mix of excitement and nerves as students donned their best attire and prepared for the influx of companies visiting to recruit. Kunal, Sakshi, Siddharth, and Anjali were among them, well-prepared to transition from mock interviews to the real thing. The placement hall was filled with booths from various companies, each one a potential gateway to their future careers. Kunal and Sakshi had meticulously planned their applications, opting for the same set of cities to ensure they could work together or at least be in the same city. "Remember our plan," Kunal said, straightening his tie. "We're aiming for the same cities, no matter what." Sakshi nodded, adjusting her blazer. "Yes, we stick together. It'll make everything so much easier."

Siddharth and Anjali joined them, looking equally determined. "Ready to ace this?" Siddharth asked, trying to lighten the mood. Anjali smiled nervously. "As ready as we'll ever be." The first round of interviews began, and the group dispersed to their respective booths. Kunal felt a surge of adrenaline as he stepped into his first interview. The atmosphere was intense, but he felt a sense of calm knowing Sakshi was nearby, facing her own set of challenges. Each day brought new companies and new opportunities. Kunal and Sakshi managed to find moments to check in with each other, offering support and encouragement.

"How did it go?" Sakshi asked one afternoon, meeting Kunal for a quick coffee break. "It went well, I think," Kunal replied, taking a sip of his coffee. "They seemed impressed with my project work. How about you?" Sakshi smiled, her eyes lighting up. "Same here. They asked a lot about my internship experience. Fingers crossed." Their friends also had their own successes and challenges. Siddharth emerged from an interview looking relieved. "That was intense, but I think I nailed it." Anjali gave him a thumbs-up. "I knew you would. Just stay confident."

As the days passed, the placement process continued to test their resilience and determination. In the evenings, they would regroup with Siddharth and Anjali, sharing their experiences and offering advice. The bond between them grew stronger as they navigated the challenges together. One night, after a particularly long day, Kunal and Sakshi managed to find some time for a short stroll. "What a tiring set of days!" Sakshi said, holding onto Kunal's arm. "These days are exhausting, but knowing we're in this together makes it bearable."

Kunal wrapped his arm around her, drawing her close. "We've got this, Sakshi. One step at a time, just like we planned." One evening, after a long day of interviews, Sakshi decided to call her parents and share her experiences with them. As she dialed the number, she felt a wave of anticipation and comfort wash over her. The phone rang a few times before her mother picked up. "Hi, Mom!" Sakshi said, trying to infuse her voice with energy despite her exhaustion. "Sakshi, my dear! How are you?" her mother's warm voice instantly made her feel at home. "I'm good, Mom. It's been a hectic week with all the placements going on, but I wanted to give you an update."

Her mother's voice was filled with curiosity and concern. "Oh, tell me everything. How are the interviews going?" Sakshi took a deep breath and started recounting her experiences. "Well, we've had a lot of companies visiting campus. I've had a few interviews already, and I think they went well. The competition is tough, but I'm doing my best." Her mother's encouraging words were a balm to her tired soul. "I'm so proud of you, Sakshi. You've always been so dedicated. Just keep doing your best, and everything will work out." Sakshi smiled, feeling a bit more at ease. "Thanks, Mom. It's been a bit overwhelming, but I'm managing. Her father's voice chimed in from the background. "How are your friends doing? Are they handling the pressure well?"

Sakshi nodded, even though they couldn't see her. "Yes, they're doing great. We've all been leaning on each other. It helps to have friends who understand what you're going through." Her mother's voice took on a reassuring tone. "Remember, Sakshi, it's not just about getting a job. It's about finding a place where you can grow and be happy. Don't stress too much about the outcome. Just focus on doing your best." Sakshi felt a tear slip down her cheek. "Thanks, Mom. I needed to hear that. Sometimes it's hard to remember the bigger picture when you're in the middle of it."

Her father added, "We believe in you, Sakshi. You've worked so hard to get here. Just keep your head up and stay positive. We're always here for you." Sakshi took a deep breath, feeling the warmth and love from her parents envelop her. "I will, Dad. Thank you both for always supporting me. I'll keep you updated on how things go." The weekend arrived, and with it came a much-needed break from the relentless placement process. Kunal, Sakshi, Siddharth, and Anjali decided to spend the day together, doing something fun to get their minds off the stress. They agreed to meet at the campus basketball court for a few friendly games, followed by a day of roaming around, shopping, and relaxing.

The sun was shining brightly as they gathered at the basketball court, dressed in casual clothes and ready to unwind. The familiar sound of the basketball bouncing on the pavement brought a sense of nostalgia and excitement. "Alright, who's ready to lose?" Siddharth joked, spinning the ball on his finger. Kunal laughed, grabbing the ball from him. "We'll see about that. Let's make it interesting." They divided into teams, with Kunal and Anjali on one side and Sakshi and Siddharth on the other. The game started with playful banter and competitive spirit, each of them eager to showcase their skills.

Sakshi made a quick pass to Siddharth, who dribbled past Kunal and scored the first basket. "Nice move!" Sakshi cheered, high-fiving Siddharth. Kunal grinned and passed the ball to Anjali. "We've got this, Anjali. Let's show them what we've got." Anjali nodded, focusing on the game. She dribbled the ball skillfully, dodging Sakshi and making a perfect shot. The game continued, filled with laughter, friendly teasing, and moments of pure fun. After playing for about an hour, they decided to take a break and head out for the day. They walked to a nearby shopping district, the excitement of the game still buzzing in their veins.

"Let's grab some snacks first," Anjali suggested. "I'm starving." They found a small cafe and ordered a variety of treats, from sandwiches to smoothies. As they sat down to eat, the conversation flowed easily, a welcome distraction from the pressures of placements. "I can't remember the last time we had this much fun," Sakshi said, taking a bite of her sandwich. After their snack, they wandered through the shops, browsing and occasionally buying small items. Sakshi spotted a pair of earrings she liked. However, Kunal suggested a different pair which caught both Sakshi's and Anjali's admiration. They agreed on Kunal's choice, appreciating his eye for detail. He picked up a quirky keychain for himself, while Anjali found a cute notebook she couldn't resist.

Their next stop was the gaming center, where they spent hours playing arcade games, laughing and cheering each other on. Kunal and Siddharth got into a competitive race on the racing simulators, while Sakshi and Anjali teamed up for a dance game, their laughter filling the room. "Okay, I admit it, you two are the dance champions," Kunal said, bowing playfully to Sakshi and Anjali after their impressive performance. The day ended with a relaxed dinner at a cozy restaurant. They shared stories, talked about their dreams, and enjoyed the simple pleasure of each other's company. The stress of the placements seemed to fade away, replaced by a sense of camaraderie and joy. As they walked back to campus under the evening sky, Sakshi slipped her hand into Kunal's. "Thank you for today. I really needed this."

Kunal squeezed her hand gently. "So did I. It was exactly what we needed." Siddharth and Anjali walked ahead, chatting animatedly, their laughter echoing in the cool night air. It had been a perfect day, a reminder that even in the midst of challenges, there was always room for joy and friendship. The new week started, and the last batch of companies visited the campus. The atmosphere was electric with anticipation, as everyone knew the placement results would be out soon. Kunal, Sakshi, Siddharth, and Anjali gave their final interviews, each hoping for the best.

A few days later, the placement results were announced. The campus was abuzz with excitement and nervous energy as students gathered to check the lists posted on the notice board. Kunal and Sakshi approached the board together, their hands tightly clasped. They had been hopeful, believing their plans would work out. But as they scanned the lists, their hearts sank. Kunal found his name first. "Kunal Singh, Bangalore," he read aloud, his voice tinged with disappointment. He turned to Sakshi, who was still searching for her name.

Sakshi's eyes widened as she found her name on the list. "Sakshi Mehra, Delhi," she said quietly, her voice barely above a whisper. They stood in stunned silence, the reality of their placements sinking in. They had been placed in cities almost on opposite ends of the country. Kunal took a deep breath, trying to keep his voice steady. "Bangalore and Delhi... how did this happen?" Sakshi's eyes filled with tears. "I don't know. We did everything we could to stay together." Siddharth and Anjali, who had also been checking the results, hurried over when they saw their friends' expressions. "What happened?" Siddharth asked, concerned.

"We got in at different companies. Kunal is going to Bangalore, and I'm going to Delhi," Sakshi explained, her voice trembling. Anjali put an arm around Sakshi, trying to offer comfort. "Oh no, I'm so sorry. That's really tough." Kunal stared at the list, feeling a mix of anger and sadness. "We planned everything so carefully. How could this happen?" Siddharth tried to stay positive. "Maybe there's a way to request a transfer? Sakshi shook her head, tears streaming down her face. "It's not that simple. These are our first jobs. And considering how good both companies are, it would be foolish to let go of this opportunity. We have to make a good impression and prove ourselves. It'll be hard to ask for transfers right away."

Kunal wrapped his arms around Sakshi, pulling her close. "We'll figure something out. We have to." The placement results had come as a shock to Kunal and Sakshi, but there was no time to dwell on it. They had only two weeks before they needed to join their new offices. The course was officially over, and everyone had to pack up and head back home before starting their respective jobs. The final day on campus arrived faster than anyone anticipated. The once bustling corridors now felt eerily quiet as students prepared to leave, each heading to different corners of the country. Kunal, Sakshi, Siddharth, and Anjali gathered their belongings and met up one last time in the common room, the weight of their impending goodbyes hanging heavy in the air.

"We've been through so much together," Anjali said, her voice thick with emotion. "It's hard to believe this is it." Siddharth nodded, trying to keep a brave face. "Yeah, but this isn't goodbye forever. We'll find ways to meet up." Kunal and Sakshi exchanged a sad smile. They had made a rough plan to meet each other as soon as they settled into their new jobs, but the uncertainty of it all was daunting. The four of them made their way to the station, their steps slow and heavy. They chatted about their memories, laughing at the good times and reminiscing about their shared struggles. Despite the somber mood, there was a sense of camaraderie and unspoken support. At the station, they found their respective platforms. Siddharth and Anjali were the first to board their train to their hometown in Kerala. They hugged Kunal and Sakshi tightly.

"Take care, guys," Siddharth said, clapping Kunal on the back. "We'll meet up soon, alright?" Anjali hugged Sakshi. "Stay strong. Let's meetup soon." As Siddharth and Anjali's train pulled away, Kunal and Sakshi were left standing together, the reality of their separation sinking in. "We'll make this work," Kunal said, his voice firm despite the sadness in his eyes. "As soon as we're settled, we'll find a way to see each other." Sakshi nodded, tears welling up in her eyes. "I know. It's just hard to say goodbye." Kunal pulled her into a tight embrace. "It's not goodbye. It's just... see you later. We have already discussed how we are going to tackle this. As soon as we get a hang of things, we are going to alternate between me coming to meet you and you coming to meet me. We got this."

They stood like that for a moment, holding on to each other as if their lives depended on it. Then, Sakshi's train was announced. She reluctantly pulled away, looking into Kunal's eyes. "I'll call you as soon as I reach home," she said, her voice trembling. "I'll be waiting," Kunal replied, forcing a smile. As Sakshi boarded the train, she turned back one last time. Kunal stood on the platform, his hand raised in a wave. She waved back, their eyes locked until the train started moving.

Kunal watched as the train slowly picked up speed, his heart heavy with a mix of love and sorrow. He kept his eyes on the train, waving until it was just a speck in the distance. While he spoke confidently about handling a long distance relationship, now that the train disappeared from view, he stood there, feeling the emptiness settle in.

ᗺᗺᗺ

14
Bright Beginnings, Bitter Ends

Two months had whisked by since Kunal and Sakshi embarked on their separate professional journeys—Kunal to Bangalore and Sakshi to Delhi. Both cities, pulsating with energy and ambition, presented a canvas of new experiences and challenges. In Bangalore, Kunal had settled into a modest 1 RK located conveniently close to his workplace—a tech startup. The apartment, though small, was tidy and functional, adorned with minimal furnishings and a few personal touches like a framed photo of Sakshi and him taken during happier times. During one of their nightly video calls, he gave Sakshi a virtual tour.

"Here's my kingdom," Kunal joked, panning his phone around the room. The walls were bare except for a small poster of a serene landscape he'd found at a local market. "It's not much, but it's home for now." Sakshi, watching from her screen, smiled warmly. "It looks cozy, Kunal. Just needs a touch of you. Maybe some more photos?" He nodded, "Definitely. I was thinking about putting up some art too. Something to make it feel less... temporary."

Sakshi, on the other hand, had found a place in a women's PG in a vibrant Delhi neighborhood, filled with cafes and boutiques. Her room, shared with another young professional, was more cramped but lively, with walls covered in posters and string lights adding a cheerful glow. During a call, as she walked Kunal through the small space filled with laughter and chatter from her roommate, she pointed out the little nook she'd made for herself. "And this is where I do all my battles," she said, showing off a small desk cluttered with books, papers, and a laptop.

Kunal laughed. "Looks like you've settled in just fine." "Yes, but I miss having you around," she replied, her voice tinged with a hint of sadness. Despite the physical distance, Kunal and Sakshi made it a point to share details of their daily routines, whether it was Sakshi's stories of the quirky café she'd discovered just around the corner from her PG or Kunal's experiences with the vibrant tech community in Bangalore. Their conversations, filled with anecdotes and shared plans, helped bridge the distance, creating a tapestry of shared experiences despite them living separate lives.

Each night, they made time for each other, their video calls becoming a digital bridge connecting their worlds. They talked about everything from mundane details like meals and weather to deeper discussions about career aspirations and future plans. As they adjusted to their new cities and jobs, these calls were their lifeline, a reminder that while much had changed, their connection remained strong, anchored in the commitment to support one another.

After weeks of planning and anticipation, Kunal's visit to Delhi marked a much-needed reunion with Sakshi. The moment he stepped off the train and saw her waiting on the platform, all the stress of their separate lives seemed to melt away. They embraced warmly, their smiles reflecting the relief and joy of being together again. Their two days in Delhi were a whirlwind of activity and laughter. Sakshi, excited to show Kunal her city, had planned a packed itinerary. They started with a visit to some of Delhi's iconic landmarks—the Red Fort and India Gate, where they took photos, joked about being tourists in their own country, and enjoyed the vibrant atmosphere.

Eating out was a special treat, with Sakshi eager to introduce Kunal to the local cuisine. They indulged in street food in Old Delhi, savoring chaats and sweet jalebis, and dined at a well-known restaurant where they had butter chicken and naan, talking about everything and nothing at all. Each meal was an opportunity to catch up, to share stories of their daily lives, and to plan for the future. Evenings were reserved for more relaxed activities. They watched movies with popcorn and soft drinks, laughing and commenting on the scenes as if they had never been apart. Shopping trips were equally laid-back, with Sakshi dragging Kunal to her favorite markets. He admired her bargaining skills and they picked out gifts for each other, small tokens to remember their time together. Walking through the crowded streets, visiting quaint cafes, and exploring little-known spots in the city, they rediscovered the ease and comfort of their relationship. It was as if the distance had only deepened their appreciation for these shared moments. Their time together flew by, and soon it was time for Kunal to return to Bangalore. The goodbye was filled with tears, hugs and promises from Sakshi to visit Bangalore as soon as possible.

Sakshi kept her promise. A month after Kunal's visit to Delhi, Sakshi planned a surprise visit to Bangalore, hoping to catch Kunal off guard and inject some spontaneity into their routine. She arrived at Bangalore railway station without Kunal's knowledge, coordinating her own travels to ensure a perfect surprise. When Kunal saw Sakshi, who waited for him outside his workplace on a Friday afternoon, his surprise turned into joy. His face lit up with a broad smile as he rushed to greet her, wrapping her in a warm embrace. The unexpected sight of her made the moment even more special. Excited to show her around his new city, Kunal had a whole itinerary in his mind the moment he realized Sakshi was there for the weekend. Their first stop was the serene Cubbon Park, where they meandered through the expansive greenery, enjoying the peaceful environment and catching up on their lives apart. Their laughter mingled with the sounds of the city as they shared stories and plans.

They then ventured to the iconic Bangalore Palace, marveling at its grand architecture and taking playful photos against the ornate backgrounds. Sakshi loved the historical charm of the palace, and Kunal was more than happy to play tour guide, detailing bits of history he had learned since moving. For lunch, Kunal introduced Sakshi to a famed local eatery where they indulged in authentic South Indian cuisine. Sakshi tried the Bangalore special—masala dosa—which Kunal claimed was unmatched elsewhere. They enjoyed the bustling atmosphere of the restaurant, immersed in the flavors and the local dialect swirling around them.

The afternoon was spent shopping in the vibrant markets of Commercial Street, where Kunal showed Sakshi his favorite spots for bargains and unique finds. Sakshi's knack for haggling impressed Kunal, and they laughed over her successful attempts to get good deals, making the afternoon a delightful adventure. Dinner was a more intimate affair at a cozy rooftop restaurant overlooking the city lights. They talked more seriously here, discussing their future, the challenges of their jobs, and how they planned to manage their long-distance relationship. The skyline of Bangalore provided a romantic backdrop to their heartfelt conversation. Kunal saved the best for last, taking Sakshi to a quiet lakeside spot he frequented when he needed to think or unwind. Here, under the starlit sky, they shared their hopes and fears, the quiet lapping of the lake waters echoing the calmness they felt in each other's presence. It was a perfect end to a perfect day. As Sakshi's train departure neared, they walked slowly to the station, savoring the last few moments together.

The first few months went by blissfully, with both of them managing to visit each other and constantly being in touch. But the reality of their demanding jobs began to encroach on Kunal and Sakshi's relationship. In Bangalore, Kunal was quickly becoming an integral part of his tech startup's expansion plans, often staying late to meet deadlines and prepare pitches for potential investors. His days, once punctuated by regular calls and messages to Sakshi, were now dominated by endless meetings and project reviews. Meanwhile, in Delhi, Sakshi faced her own set of challenges. Her role in a leading consultancy firm meant dealing with high-profile clients and managing complex projects that demanded not just her time but also her full cognitive commitment. Her phone, which once buzzed with Kunal's name, now lay silent beside her during long strategy sessions and client meetings.

The shift was gradual but undeniable. Initially, missed calls were followed by quick apologies and promises to catch up soon. However, as weeks turned into months, these promises became harder to fulfill. Texts went unanswered for hours, and scheduled video calls were postponed or canceled altogether. One evening, Kunal tried to initiate a call, hoping to recreate some of their old routines. But the call went unanswered, and when Sakshi finally returned it hours later, the conversation was brief and distracted.

"I'm sorry, Kunal. It's just been so hectic," Sakshi explained, her voice tinged with exhaustion. "I had back-to-back meetings, and then something came up with a client. I didn't even see the time." Kunal tried to mask his disappointment. "It's okay, I understand. We're both just... swamped, I guess."

The frequency of their communication dwindled further as Sakshi's project deadlines loomed and Kunal's startup entered a critical phase of development. Their conversations, once filled with laughter and shared dreams, now often revolved around the stress of work and the logistics of navigating their increasingly incompatible schedules.

Tensions began to surface during one of their rare calls when Kunal expressed his frustration. "It feels like we're only talking about work these days. What happened to us talking about everything and anything?"

Sakshi, feeling equally frustrated by the distance but overwhelmed by her responsibilities, replied sharply, "What do you want me to say, Kunal? It's not like I have a lot of free time either."

Their calls, once the highlight of their days, started to feel like a burden—a reminder of the growing gap between their lived realities. Heated discussions became more frequent, with both feeling the strain of maintaining a connection that was once effortless.

The tension that had been building between Kunal and Sakshi reached its peak one late evening when both were exhausted from a long day's work. Kunal, feeling particularly isolated after another exhausting day at work, dialed Sakshi hoping to find some comfort in their conversation. However, Sakshi, overwhelmed by her own deadlines, answered the call already fraught with stress.

"Hey," Kunal started, his voice heavy, "I really needed to hear your voice today. It's been rough."

Sakshi, sorting through a pile of documents, responded distractedly, "Kunal, can we talk later? I'm buried in reports and this new project is driving me up the wall."

Her terse tone stung Kunal, who had hoped for a few moments of escape from his own pressures. "Sakshi, it's always later with us these days. When do we actually get to just talk?"

"I don't know, Kunal! Not now, I can't do this now," Sakshi snapped back, her patience worn thin by her unrelenting schedule.

Kunal's frustration boiled over. "It's like I don't even know what's going on with you anymore. We used to share everything. Now, I feel like I'm just another item on your to-do list!"

Sakshi's voice rose, matching his frustration. "And you think I don't miss you? You think I don't want things to be different? I'm trying to hold onto my job here, Kunal. I'm trying to secure a future—for both of us!"

The words hung heavy in the air. Kunal, feeling a mix of anger and helplessness, retorted, "If we can't even find time to talk, what kind of future are we even trying to build? It feels like we're just drifting apart!"

"Maybe we are," Sakshi said quietly, her anger giving way to sadness. "Maybe that's just what happens when two people want different things. Or maybe, it's just too hard to keep this going from so far apart."

Stung by her words, Kunal felt a deep, hollow pain in his chest. "Is that what you want then? To just end things because it's too hard?"

"I don't know, Kunal! I don't have all the answers," Sakshi replied, her voice breaking with emotion. "I just know I can't do this right now. I can't fight like this anymore."

With those words, the call ended abruptly, leaving a silence that was louder than the words they had exchanged.

❧❧❧

15

The Silence After Us

Days turned into a week with no calls or messages between Kunal and Sakshi. Each waited for the other to reach out, their deep-seated pride and pain forming a barrier neither felt ready to breach. This silence marked the longest they had ever gone without speaking since they had first met. As each day passed, the silence deepened, the chasm between them growing wider and more profound. Kunal stared at his phone night after night, the weight of unspoken words pressing heavily on his chest. Memories of their laughter and shared dreams played like a loop in his mind, starkly contrasting with their current reality. The urge to dial her number was overwhelming, yet fear of rejection or another argument kept him from pressing 'call.'

Meanwhile, Sakshi found herself glancing at her silent phone more often than she cared to admit. The quiet buzz of notifications from work and friends couldn't fill the void left by Kunal's absence. She longed to hear his voice, to laugh about nothing in particular, yet the pain from their last argument lingered, a bitter aftertaste that made her hesitate. The strain wasn't just emotional but began to seep into their everyday lives, clouding their thoughts during meetings and solitary meals. Their shared past, once a source of strength, now seemed like a series of missed opportunities and misunderstandings. As the week stretched on, the realization that this could be the end of what had once seemed unbreakable became a haunting possibility neither wanted to face.

Kunal, burdened by the weight of their prolonged silence, decided it was time to bridge the gap physically. The strain of not hearing from Sakshi had left him restless, and he knew he needed to see her face-to-face if there was any hope of mending their relationship. On a whim, driven more by his heart than his head, he booked a flight to Delhi, his decision unannounced and unplanned. Landing in Delhi, his heart was a mix of anticipation and anxiety. He traveled directly from the airport to Sakshi's new apartment that she had recently moved into. He kept rehearsing apologies and the right words to say, hoping that seeing each other might reignite the warmth that had been overshadowed by recent conflicts.

When he arrived at her doorstep, his knock was hesitant, but the urgency of his mission lent him enough resolve. Sakshi answered the door, her expression a mixture of surprise and wariness. The moment she saw Kunal, a complex flurry of emotions passed over her face. "Kunal? What are you doing here?" she asked, her voice tinged with a mix of confusion and a hint of relief. "I couldn't just wait and do nothing," Kunal explained, stepping inside as she motioned him to come in. "We've been apart and silent for too long, and I thought... maybe we could talk. Really talk, and figure things out together."

Sakshi nodded, albeit with a hint of hesitation, leading him into the small living room that felt far too intimate, given the situation. They sat down, the physical space between them on the sofa mirroring the emotional distance that had grown between them. The conversation started awkwardly, with both tiptoeing around the real issues, but as they warmed up, the deeper frustrations began to surface. Kunal expressed his loneliness and the pain of not being part of her daily life anymore. Sakshi shared her pressures and the overwhelming demands of her job that left her drained and often unavailable.

As they talked, there were moments when it seemed like they might rediscover their old rhythm. Laughs were shared, old inside jokes revisited, and for a brief moment, it felt like they could return to the old days. But as the initial relief of reconnection faded, the reality of their situation set in. "It's not just about missing calls or not texting," Sakshi finally said, her voice steady but sad. "It's about how we're growing in different directions. We need to think about what's really best for us." Kunal knew she was right, but accepting it was hard. "I know," he responded quietly, "But isn't there something worth fighting for? Can't we try to find a way to work through this?" As the evening progressed, Kunal and Sakshi ventured out for dinner, hoping a change of scenery might lighten the atmosphere. They chose a quiet restaurant, a place away from the hustle of the city, where they could talk without distractions. Initially, the familiar act of sharing a meal brought a sense of normalcy, reminiscing about past dates and happier times.

However, as the conversation deepened, the old issues that had driven a wedge between them began to resurface. Kunal, optimistic at the start, found himself pushing for commitments Sakshi wasn't ready to make, given the uncertainty of their future paths. Sakshi, increasingly feeling the pressure, struggled to balance her affection for Kunal with the stark realities of her career ambitions and personal growth. "I just think we need more time," Kunal suggested, reaching across the table to hold her hand. "Time to adjust to everything, to find a middle ground."

Sakshi withdrew slightly, her expression torn. "Kunal, it's not about time. It's about us changing. I'm not the same person I was in college, and neither are you. We are travelling down different paths and maybe it's time we accept that." Her eyes started welling up as soon as she said that. This statement hung heavily between them, the implications clear and cutting. The rest of the meal passed in near silence, the tension palpable. After dinner, they walked back to Sakshi's apartment in a somber mood, each lost in their thoughts.

Back at her apartment, the unresolved feelings and the stress of the visit came to a head. Kunal, unable to let go of the hope that they could resolve their differences, pressed Sakshi for a clearer answer about where they stood. "Sakshi, please, I believe we still have something left worth fighting for. We can figure this out, together," he pleaded, his voice laced with desperation. Sakshi, her patience fraying under the weight of her own conflicted emotions, responded more sharply than intended. "Kunal, you're not listening. I think we both need space to grow on our own, to build our careers without feeling guilty about not being available for each other."

This exchange escalated quickly, their words fueled by hurt and frustration, leading to a heated argument that neither had wanted. Voices raised, old grievances aired, and it became clear that their attempts at reconciliation were crumbling. The night ended with him leaving her apartment, the cold night air reflecting the chill that had settled in his heart.

The continuous strain from her personal conflicts began to visibly affect Sakshi's professional life. Once known for her meticulous attention to detail and sharp analytical skills, she found herself increasingly absent-minded and disengaged during meetings, missing key information, and falling short of her usual performance standards. Her colleagues, who had come to depend on her reliability and insight, started to notice her diminished enthusiasm and occasional oversights.

Realizing the detrimental impact her emotional turmoil was having on her career, Sakshi acknowledged the need for a respite—a chance to step back from the relentless pressures and reassess her priorities. After a candid conversation with her manager, who expressed concern over her recent dip in performance, she was encouraged to take some time off. Grateful for the understanding, Sakshi decided a visit home might restore her equilibrium. She booked her journey back to her home, seeking the solace and unconditional support only family could offer. She anticipated that the familiar environment, filled with memories and the comforting presence of loved ones, would provide a safe space to decompress and sort through the tangled emotions plaguing her.

At home, surrounded by the affectionate embraces of her family and the soothing rhythms of a slower-paced life, Sakshi hoped to rediscover her inner calm and clarity. This break from her daily routines in Delhi was not just a physical escape but a mental and emotional sanctuary, allowing her the space to reflect on her personal and professional life and how best to navigate the challenges ahead. After a few restorative days with her family, Sakshi returned to Delhi feeling more centered and clear-headed. The time away had provided her with not just rest, but also perspective—a chance to view her relationship with Kunal without the immediate cloud of emotion and stress.

As she settled back into her apartment, the quiet moments allowed her to reflect deeply on the path she and Kunal were on. The distance, the continuous misunderstandings, and the recent intense arguments illuminated a troubling pattern that seemed only to deepen with time. More critically, she recognized how these personal stresses were beginning to bleed into her professional life, threatening the career she had worked so hard to build. Sakshi revisited their last conversations, the unresolved issues, and their painful, circular arguments. Each recollection confirmed her growing belief that their relationship, in its current state, was unsustainable. It wasn't just the physical distance that was the issue, but the emotional drift that had grown between them, exacerbated by their conflicting schedules and priorities.

With a heavy heart but a firm resolve, Sakshi decided that it was time to face the hard truth. She concluded that continuing their relationship under such strain was unfair to both of them. It wasn't just about the lack of time or the geographical distance; it was about the fundamental changes in their lives and selves that no longer aligned as they once had.

Determined to handle the situation with as much care and respect as possible, Sakshi planned a video call with Kunal. She intended to communicate her decision clearly and compassionately, hoping to preserve the love and respect that had initially brought them together. In her heart, she felt that ending their romantic relationship was the kindest thing she could do—for both of them—allowing them to focus on their individual growth without the constant stress of trying to bridge a gap that seemed to widen with each passing day.

When Kunal saw Sakshi's name flash on his screen after days of thick, suffocating silence, a surge of hope washed over him. His heart skipped as he swiped to answer, his voice shaky yet filled with a warm, welcoming tone, "Sakshi! I've missed you. How are you?"

Sakshi's face, appearing on the screen, carried a stoic calmness, a stark contrast to the emotional turmoil evident in her eyes. "Hi, Kunal," she said, her voice steady but her lips trembling slightly. "We need to talk. Seriously this time." Kunal's heart sank; her tone, her expression, it was all too formal, too grave. "Of course, I'm listening," he responded, trying to mask his growing apprehension with a forced smile.

Sakshi paused, gathering her thoughts, her gaze drifting away before locking back on the screen. "Kunal, these past months have been...challenging. Not just busy, but emotionally draining for both of us. We've been hanging by a thread, holding onto moments that are becoming rarer by the day." Kunal felt a tightness in his chest. "I know it's been tough, Sakshi, but isn't that part of being together? We work through the tough times, no matter how bad it gets. We've always talked about how our love is stronger than any challenge." Sakshi sighed, a sound so heavy it seemed to carry the weight of all their unsaid words. "Love isn't our problem, Kunal. It never was. It's everything else – the distance, our careers, our futures. We're pulling each other in opposite directions, and it's tearing us apart."

Kunal leaned forward, his voice desperate, "But we can fix it, Sakshi. We can make plans, see each other more—" "Can we, Kunal?" Sakshi cut him off, her voice rising in frustration. "Or do we keep pretending that the next visit will solve everything? Each time we say goodbye, a part of me feels lost. We argue, we make up, but nothing changes. We're stuck in this loop, and it's hurting us both." Kunal's face showed his turmoil, caught between anger and sorrow. "So, what? That's it? You want to end this?" "It's not about what I want," Sakshi's voice softened, her own conflict clear in her tearful eyes. "It's about what we need. And right now, it feels like we need space to grow individually. We're just...holding each other back."

"That's not true!" Kunal's voice broke, his emotions bubbling to the surface. "You're not holding me back, Sakshi. You're the reason I push myself!" "And yet here we are, fighting more than we're loving," Sakshi whispered, her words slicing through the air with a painful accuracy. "I'm tired, Kunal. Tired of the misunderstandings, the missed calls, the lack of communication... It's like we're in a relationship with our phones, not each other." Kunal rubbed his face, struggling to find words. His voice, when he spoke, was choked. "I love you, Sakshi. Isn't that enough?"

"Love should make us better, Kunal. But look at us—we're just shadows of who we used to be, shadows of who we want to be. I think...I think we need to let go. For us." Kunal felt as if the ground had shifted beneath him. "So, this is goodbye? After all we've been through?" "It's the hardest choice I've ever made," Sakshi admitted, a tear rolling down her cheek. "But sometimes, loving someone means letting them go." The finality in her voice was unmistakable. Kunal tried to speak, but no words came out. He just nodded, numb and disbelieving. Sakshi wiped her tears, her voice a mere whisper now. "Goodbye, Kunal. I wish you all the happiness in the world." All Kunal could manage to utter was, "Sak... We..."

With a click, the screen went dark. Kunal sat there, staring at the blank phone, the silence deafening him. The room felt emptier, the world a shade grayer. He had lost not just his love, but his best friend. As reality set in, he buried his face in his hands, the ache in his heart deepening with the quiet that followed.

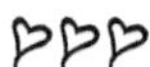

16

The Quiet After the Storm

6 months had passed since Sakshi's image vanished from Kunal's phone screen, leaving behind a silence that was louder than any sound ever. Hiss apartment felt more like a shell than a home. Where there used to be laughter and chatter, now there was just a deep, unsettling quiet. His once neat and tidy space was now cluttered and neglected, much like his appearance. He'd stopped shaving regularly, and his hair was unkempt. The vibrant life he once led seemed like a distant memory. Kunal's withdrawal from work was becoming noticeable. He often missed days, and when he did show up, his lack of focus and disinterest worried his colleagues. They tried to reach out, but he brushed off their concerns with vague excuses.

The nights were the hardest. Lying awake, Kunal would scroll through his phone, pausing at photos of him and Sakshi—vacations they took, dinners, random selfies from lazy afternoons. Each image, each message exchange was a sharp jab reminding him of what he'd lost. Sometimes he'd replay their last conversations, torturing himself with the finality of their words, the coldness that had crept into their last exchanges. Despite everything, he respected Sakshi's decision to end things and restrained himself from calling her, though the temptation nagged at him constantly. He missed her deeply, not just as his girlfriend but as his closest friend, the one he'd always turned to when things got tough.

Kunal's family started to worry too. He wasn't calling them much anymore, and when he did, his voice was flat, his words sparse. He assured them he was just busy with work, but the strain in his voice was hard to disguise.

Late at night, he would sit on his balcony, looking out over a city that didn't sleep, feeling a loneliness so profound it scared him. He had almost given in to the urge to check Sakshi's social media profiles several times, hoping maybe just seeing her online might lessen the ache. But every time he hovered over her profiles, he pulled back. And on the rare occasions he did click through, there was nothing new to see. Her accounts were just as silent as his apartment—no updates, no photos, nothing. It seemed she too had withdrawn, cutting off her digital presence, leaving no trace of how she was coping or what she was feeling. This silence from her side only deepened Kunal's sense of isolation, reminding him that the disconnection was complete. This new routine was wearing him down—his spirit, his will to engage with the world outside. The breakup had taken more than just Sakshi from his life; it seemed to have taken his very essence, leaving him to wonder if he'd ever feel whole again.

One quiet evening, Kunal was cleaning out a drawer that was overflowing with piles of paperwork from his office. A small attempt to distract himself. His hand brushed against something unexpected—a small, wrapped gift that Sakshi had given him but he had never opened, saving it for a "special day." The sight of her familiar handwriting on the wrapping sent a sharp pang through his heart. Curious and masochistic, he tore it open, finding a custom-made keychain inside, engraved with their initials and the date of their first anniversary.

Holding the keychain, he felt the dam break within him. The weight of the silent apartment, the unreturned smiles at work, the cold dinners—everything hit him at once. He slid to the floor, the keychain clenched in his fist, and for the first time since the breakup, Kunal allowed himself to truly break down. Tears came first, quiet and continuous, then grew into deep, heaving sobs that echoed off the empty walls. It was in this moment, surrounded by the scattered contents of his life, that Kunal felt the full extent of his isolation. He realized that no amount of self-imposed solitude could erase the pain; it only deepened it. His heartache had seeped into every corner of his life, tainting everything with sadness. This realization was his breaking point, the stark acknowledgment that he couldn't navigate his grief alone. He needed help, he needed to connect with someone—anyone—before he lost himself entirely in the shadows of his broken heart. And at that point of time, his resolve to never disturb Sakshi broke. With shaking hands, he picked up his phone and dialled her number. "Hello." The moment he heard Sakshi's voice, tears ran down his face, his breathing got faster and he could barely talk. Sakshi was in a terrible situation here. If she spoke to him, she feared she wouldn't be able to stay away from him. And if she just disconnected the call, she worried whether Kunal would be ok. In a split second, she added Sidd to the call and kept her phone away. Siddharth, initially not able to make out what was going on, heard Kunal on the other end, crying his heart out. After what seemed like an eternity, Sidd was finally able to calm him down.

Months of grappling with the shadow of despair had left Kunal exhausted, both emotionally and physically. The unwavering darkness that followed him seemed endless, yet a part of him—a quiet, persistent voice—urged him to seek light, to find a semblance of the person he used to be before the heartbreak.

It began with small, almost imperceptible steps. One morning, he found himself standing in front of the mirror, staring at the reflection of a man he barely recognized. The unkempt hair, the hollow eyes, and the unkempt beard were not just marks of his suffering but reminders of his neglect towards himself. With a deep, cleansing breath, Kunal reached for his razor and grooming kit, each stroke clearing away not just facial hair but layers of pain that had started to feel like a second skin. It was not just about looking presentable; it was about feeling alive again, about taking back some control from the chaos that had engulfed him.

Reinvigorated by this act of self-care, Kunal returned to his job with a renewed focus. His workspace, once cluttered with scattered papers and empty coffee cups, gradually transformed back into the organized and efficient setup it had been. Colleagues who had grown used to his sullen silence and distant gazes now noticed a slight shift. There were small smiles, brief exchanges about projects, and gradually, Kunal began to reclaim his reputation as a diligent worker, his insights and dedication reflecting a man determined to excel despite his personal turmoil.

Despite these efforts at work, the evenings remained difficult, the loneliness palpable as he returned to an empty apartment. The silence was often too loud, filled with echoes of a past that was too painful to remember yet impossible to forget. However, Kunal knew that healing was not just about changing his surroundings or improving his professional life; it was about mending the emotional tears. In an attempt to reconnect with parts of his life that had brought him joy before the sorrow, Kunal dusted off his old guitar, an instrument that had once been a source of solace and expression. His fingers were stiff, his playing rusty, but each note, each melody was a step towards healing, a nod to the resilience of the human spirit.

And then, one evening, as he was strumming a particularly melancholic tune, a knock sounded at his door. The unexpected interruption startled him; visitors had become a rarity in his life of isolation. With a curious mix of anxiety and hope, Kunal set his guitar aside and walked to the door. Peering through the peephole, his heart leapt with a mix of surprise and relief—it was Sid, his old friend, standing there with a cautious but warm smile. As he opened the door, Sid's presence felt like a breath of fresh air into the stifling stagnation that had filled Kunal's apartment. "I've been worried about you, man," Sid said as he stepped inside, his voice laced with concern but also a hint of cheer. "Thought I'd come and check on you. Maybe drag you out for some fresh air and good food, huh? You look like you could use it."

Kunal, overwhelmed by this gesture of friendship, felt a warmth spread through him—a reminder that he was not alone, that there were still people who cared. This visit might have been simple, perhaps mundane in the eyes of an outsider, but for Kunal, it was a lifeline thrown at a time when he was just learning to swim again in the turbulent waters of life. It was not just the end of a chapter marked by despair but the beginning of a new one filled with tentative hope and the promise of recovery. The cafe buzzed with the soft hum of afternoon chatter as Kunal and Siddharth settled into a cozy corner, the familiar scent of coffee weaving through the air. Though it had only been months since they'd last met, the distance of those months felt much longer, laden with the weight of change.

Sidd broke the silence, his voice laced with concern. "Heard from Anjali that things have been rough," he started cautiously, his eyes searching Kunal's. "She mentioned Sakshi's having a tough time too... says she misses you, but she feels breaking up was the right thing. How are you holding up, man?" Kunal took a deep breath, his fingers wrapped tightly around his coffee mug. "It's been tough, Sidd. I mean, it just started to feel like we were making each other miserable instead of happy. Our paths were just too different. It hurt, knowing we loved each other but couldn't make it work because of everything else acting against us."

Sidd nodded, his expression softening. "Yeah, I can only imagine, man. But you know, sometimes love isn't enough by itself. You both needed more than what you could give each other under the circumstances." The conversation eased into memories of college, laughter filling the gaps of silence, but inevitably, it swung back to Kunal's current struggles. "It's just... all these changes, they've hit me hard. I find myself wondering if I lost more than just a girlfriend. I lost my confidante, my closest friend," Kunal confessed, his voice a mixture of sadness and reflection.

"You did, and it's okay to feel this void, Kunal. But you've also got to think about healing, man. You can't let this breakup define your life," Sidd urged gently. "Maybe start slow, get back into the world, you know? Doesn't have to be anything serious, just... reconnect with life again." Kunal smiled wryly, "Dating again, huh? I can't even think about it to be honest." "Yeah, but who says it has to be about dating right away? Just meet new people, pick up some old hobbies, or maybe find new ones. Life's about these little steps, man. And who knows? You might end up surprising yourself," Sidd replied with a grin.

Their conversation meandered through the practicalities of moving forward, each piece of advice from Sidd punctuated by genuine care and understanding. As they stood to leave, the cool evening air felt like a fresh start, a subtle push towards new beginnings. "Thanks, Sidd. It means a lot, you coming all the way and giving me that push," Kunal said, genuine gratitude warming his voice. "Always here for you, buddy. Just remember, it's one step at a time. And hey, let's not let months pass before we meet up again, alright?" Sidd replied, clapping Kunal on the back as they parted ways.

Kunal walked away with a lighter heart, the seeds of recovery sown in the span of a heartfelt conversation. Was it indeed time to start anew? To slowly rebuild from the emotional turmoil and find himself again in the process. Could he finally let go and move on?

ᐅᐅᐅ

17

Swipe Right or Swipe Left?

After his heart-to-heart with Sidd, Kunal felt a spark of motivation to actively mend the fragments of his life. It wasn't a sudden transformation, but a gradual shift towards reclaiming the life he'd put on hold. His resolve to heal and grow stronger in the aftermath of his breakup led him to make more meaningful efforts in every aspect of his daily routine.

Kunal's engagement at work, which had already seen a slight improvement, began to intensify. He participated more actively in team meetings and office events, no longer just going through the motions but contributing ideas that reminded everyone of his potential and passion for his work. These small achievements at work served as daily reminders that he could excel and find satisfaction in his professional life once more.

Conversations with his family became more frequent and involved. He shared more about his days, asked about theirs, and found comfort in the simple exchange of familial love and concern. These calls helped bridge the physical distance between them, weaving a stronger bond that buoyed his spirits.

Though Kunal, Anjali, and Sidd were in different cities, their communication grew more regular. Their phone calls were filled with updates, shared experiences, and the occasional necessary venting session. These interactions, though virtual, played a crucial role in Kunal's support system, offering him a sense of continuity and connection.

On his own, Kunal rediscovered solace in solitude through his old hobbies. He resumed reading, losing himself in novels that transported him to different realms, away from the echoes of his own troubles. Walks in the park became a ritual, the fresh air and quiet paths providing a backdrop for reflection and a gradual return to inner peace.

These activities, both social and solitary, didn't erase the pain or fill the void left by Sakshi's absence entirely, but they provided Kunal with necessary distractions and moments of joy. They were essential steps in a journey of rediscovery—of his strengths, interests, and the relationships that mattered.

This period in Kunal's life was marked by a gentle rediscovery of himself and the world around him. It was about understanding that while some days were undoubtedly harder than others, each effort, no matter how small, was a step towards a future where his past heartbreak did not define him. With each day, he felt more grounded, more like someone ready to face life's complexities with a renewed spirit and resilience.

Encouraged by Siddharth's advice, Kunal decided it was time to explore new beginnings. With a mix of trepidation and a faint spark of hope, he downloaded a couple of dating apps, creating profiles that he hoped would reflect who he was—someone still healing but ready to move forward. As he filled out his interests and selected photos that showed his smiling face, there was a surreal feeling to the process. It was as if he was stepping into a new chapter, one that he never expected to write so soon.

The act of setting up his dating profiles was bittersweet. Each click and swipe was a reminder of the void left by Sakshi, yet it also represented a possibility—perhaps not of finding love immediately, but at least of connecting with others who might understand, or share, similar experiences. As he browsed through potential matches, Kunal felt a strange blend of excitement and guilt. He wondered if it was too soon, or if he was somehow betraying the memories of what he had with Sakshi.

Despite these doubts, Kunal pressed on, driven by a deeper understanding that life had to continue and that stagnation was not an option. His first few interactions were awkward, conversations that often felt forced and stilted as he tried to engage with strangers. The small talk, the getting-to-know-you questions—it all felt so mundane yet necessary, a ritual of modern dating that one couldn't bypass.

As Kunal navigated the uncertain waters of new relationships, each date brought its own set of dynamics and lessons. Some evenings were lackluster from the start, with stilted conversations that reminded Kunal just how challenging it could be to forge a connection with someone new. These dates often ended with a polite handshake or a brief hug, a silent agreement that there was no spark worth pursuing further.

On other occasions, Kunal met women with whom he shared genuine laughs and interesting conversations. These dates were different; they had a rhythm and an ease that surprised him, moments where he could almost forget the lingering sadness in the back of his mind. He met Maya, a graphic designer whose passion for art sparked lively debates and shared smiles. There was also Alisha, a friend of Sidd's, who happened to be in Bangalore around that time. Sidd, who was in Bangalore for a couple of days for a meeting, decided to introduce Alisha and Kunal to each other. Alisha was a fellow tech enthusiast, whose stories about startup life and mutual challenges in the tech industry led to an evening that extended well beyond their planned dinner.

Despite these promising interactions, Kunal found himself grappling with an internal conflict. With Maya, he enjoyed the artistic insight and the refreshing perspective she brought to things he'd never paid much attention to. Their walks through local art galleries were filled with a lightness that Kunal hadn't felt in months. Yet, as he lay in bed after those dates, his mind wandered back to Sakshi, to the deep conversations and the profound connection they had shared, which he couldn't fully replicate or replace.

With Alisha, the connection was intellectually stimulating, discussing the latest tech trends and sharing insights from their respective fields. She was engaging and understanding, often texting Kunal encouraging words before a big presentation or a stressful meeting. Yet, this camaraderie, as comforting as it was, highlighted what Kunal felt was missing—a deeper emotional bond that he still associated only with Sakshi.

This pattern of fleeting highs followed by introspective lows began to wear on him. He found himself in a tug-of-war between the desire to move forward and the guilt and loyalty he felt towards his past with Sakshi. Each promising date left him more confused; he appreciated the company and the newness of these relationships, but they also served as mirrors, reflecting what was no longer his.

Kunal's heart wasn't in it to lead anyone on, knowing his own heart was still in recovery. After several weeks of this push and pull, he had a particularly reflective night where he realized he couldn't fully invest himself in these new relationships. He was transparent with Maya and Alisha, explaining his situation without going into too many details. "I value what we've shared, and you deserve someone who can give you their all," he told them, his voice laced with a mix of respect and regret. While Maya failed to understand his inner turmoil and moved on quickly, Alisha tried to convince him to give it more time, suggesting that feelings can grow and heal with patience.

They were at a small, intimate cafe they both favored. The place had become a comforting setting for their growing acquaintance. Alisha's understanding nature and her patience with his hesitations had encouraged Kunal to open up more than he had initially intended.

As they sipped their coffee, the conversation naturally drifted towards deeper waters. Alisha's keen perception didn't miss the slight hesitations Kunal exhibited whenever the conversation veered towards future plans or deeper commitments.

"You seem a bit guarded whenever we touch on anything too serious. I hope you feel comfortable telling me if something's bothering you," Alisha said gently, her eyes full of concern.

Kunal sighed, the internal battle evident on his face. "Alisha, I've really enjoyed our time together, but there's a part of me that keeps holding back. I'm still tethered to a past relationship, and it's been hard. It was a perfect and beautiful phase of my life that I haven't yet let go of. I don't want to end up hurting you because I can't fully commit," he confessed, looking earnestly into her eyes. He felt he should open up and mention everything about Sakshi to Alisha, but decided against it. He felt he was not ready to talk about it and mentioned the same to Alisha.

She reached out, touching his hand lightly. "I appreciate your honesty, Kunal. It's clear you've been through something serious and I also understand why you don't want to go into too many details. But maybe this—what we have—isn't about diving headfirst into something serious. Why not just take it as it comes? Give it some time, and see how things evolve."

Kunal's eyes reflected his turmoil, appreciating her words but conflicted within. "I want to, I really do. But I'm scared of not being able to give you what you deserve. What if I can't move past my old feelings?"

"It's natural to feel that way," Alisha reassured him, squeezing his hand. "No one starts a new relationship completely unscarred. It's about growing together, learning about each other, and giving yourself permission to be happy again. You don't have to be a hundred percent sure right now. Just be open to the possibility."

Kunal paused, taking in her words. Her compassion and patience made him consider the possibility of allowing himself to heal through this new connection. "Maybe you're right. I shouldn't let my past hold back a potential future. Let's take things slowly, one step at a time."

Alisha smiled, a warm, reassuring smile that eased some of the tightness in Kunal's chest. "That's all I'm asking. Let's just enjoy getting to know each other, with no pressure for more until you're ready."

As they left the cafe, Kunal felt a weight lift slightly off his shoulders. He was still unsure about many things, but Alisha's understanding had given him a glimmer of hope. Perhaps, in time, he could find the strength to move past his past and embrace whatever lay ahead with her.

Weeks had passed since Kunal and Alisha's candid conversation at the cafe, and their relationship had evolved into a comforting, if somewhat uneven, rhythm. Alisha's affection was palpable, expressed through her thoughtful gestures and heartfelt words that often left Kunal feeling both cherished and overwhelmed. She found joy in his laughter, listened with intent to his stories, and eagerly planned their next adventures together. Her proactive involvement in his life clearly signaled her deepening feelings.

Kunal appreciated Alisha's presence and genuinely relished the moments they shared. Alisha embodied what one might consider ideal traits in a partner—compassion, intelligence, and a resonance with his own thoughts and feelings. Yet, despite these harmonious interactions, each smile and shared laugh was shadowed by a lingering sadness within Kunal. He genuinely liked her—more than he had expected—but the spark that should have been kindled by such compatibility was conspicuously absent. Instead, a void within him persisted, a silent testament to a love not yet relinquished.

Despite his inner turmoil, Kunal made concerted efforts to not let his past overshadow the present. He recognized Alisha's needs and aspirations within the relationship and pushed himself to meet them as best as he could. Alisha, for her part, seemed to understand intuitively when Kunal needed space or when he needed encouragement. Her gestures, like organizing a surprise birthday party for him and showing up unexpectedly at his office with his favorite lunch, were not just acts of affection but also her way of showing commitment.

Their bond deepened during these shared experiences, yet Kunal's heart remained a battleground of emotions. One evening, while they were taking a walk at Cubbon park, Alisha turned to him with a soft smile and a question that caught him off-guard. "You seem distant sometimes, lost in thoughts. What haunts you, Kunal?" Her voice was gentle, probing not out of curiosity but out of a desire to share his burdens.

Kunal hesitated, then opened up about his previous relationship, but he refrained from mentioning Sakshi's name. Alisha listened, her hand finding his in a comforting squeeze, encouraging him to live in the moment and to explore the possibilities of their growing connection without the shadow of his past looming over them.

Yet, Kunal's internal conflict did not wane. He found himself constantly comparing the depth of his past love with the budding relationship with Alisha. Each of Alisha's perfect gestures, each moment of perceived happiness, was weighed against a memory, a past that refused to fade. He felt guilty for his inability to fully engage, to give Alisha the love she so freely offered him.

One particularly reflective evening, as they shared a quiet dinner at Alisha's place, Kunal's emotions spilled over. The walls adorned with her artwork, the cozy ambiance she had created—it all felt bittersweet. "Alisha, you do so much, and I... I feel like I'm always holding back," he confessed, his voice tinged with frustration and sorrow.

Alisha reached across the table, her touch reassuring. "Kunal, it's okay to feel unsure. Don't force yourself to forget your past. Maybe we don't need to rush this. Let's just enjoy these moments, without any pressure."

Kunal nodded, grateful for her understanding yet tormented by his own doubts.

This went on for a few more weeks. Alisha was getting more and more invested in the relationship while Kunal struggled to make progress. One fine day, they met up after work for a quick catchup. They walked through a lane that had a pond next to it. Alisha's laughter was ringing clear in the crisp air and Kunal found himself watching her with a mix of admiration and sorrow. She was pointing at a clumsy duck waddling near the pond, her delight infectious. Kunal smiled, but the action felt mechanical. It was at that moment, watching Alisha's unabashed mirth, that he realized the unfairness of the situation.

That night, back in his quiet apartment, Kunal sat down with a heavy heart. He needed to make sense of the tumult within him, to understand why the presence of someone as wonderful as Alisha couldn't fill the void left by Sakshi. It was something within him, a barrier he hadn't realized was there until now. Perhaps he was holding onto an ideal, an idea of love that had been irrevocably shaped by his relationship with Sakshi. He poured himself a drink, a rare indulgence, and allowed his thoughts to drift. The memories of Sakshi were less painful now, more a bittersweet echo of the past than the sharp pangs of initial grief. Yet, her absence was a constant presence, an empty space no one else seemed able to fill. Perhaps, he simply wasn't ready to let anyone else in, not fully, not yet.

The realization was both liberating and painful. Kunal understood that stepping back from this relationship with Alisha; it was an acknowledgment of his need to heal fully. He needed time—time to rediscover who he was outside of a relationship, time to love himself enough so that one day, he could love someone else without reservations.

The decision weighed heavy on him as he picked up his phone to call Alisha. She answered with her usual cheer, which only tightened the knot in his stomach. "Alisha, we need to talk," Kunal began, his voice steady but softer than usual. He explained his feelings, his appreciation for her, and his recent epiphanies about his emotional state. Alisha listened quietly, her silence a blanket over the phone line.

When she finally spoke, her voice was understanding but tinged with sadness. "Kunal, I'm glad you're honest with me, and I respect your decision. I care about you deeply, and I want what's best for you, even if that means taking a step back. This is not going to be an easy task for me. I was actually... falling for you quite badly. But I understand. I understand your point."

They agreed to remain friends, a testament to the genuine affection and respect that had grown between them. As Kunal hung up the phone, the quiet of his apartment enveloped him once more.

It was a familiar silence, but this time it was tinged with a new sense of understanding and acceptance. He stood at the window, gazing out at the city lights that seemed to twinkle with possibilities and paths yet to be explored.

In this moment of solitude, Kunal felt a profound shift within himself. The conversation with Alisha had not just marked the end of a budding relationship but had also crystallized a vital truth in his mind. He was simply not ready to dive into another relationship, not yet. His heart, still shadowed by past hurts and memories, needed more time to find its rhythm again.

Kunal allowed himself to reflect on the past months. Each attempt at dating, each interaction had taught him something about himself. He had learned that moving on wasn't just about filling a void left by someone else; it was about understanding and nurturing oneself, about healing the parts that were broken, and about knowing when to hold back.

He appreciated Alisha and the brief moments of happiness they shared, but he recognized that his happiness could not be contingent on another person. It needed to come from within, from a place of self-awareness and self-compassion. This realization wasn't easy. It came with its own pain and loneliness, but it also carried a promise of growth and deeper emotional resilience.

Kunal decided to focus on himself, to embrace the solitude that had once felt like an enemy. He planned to reconnect with his passions, those parts of his life that had been sidelined in his pursuit of romantic fulfillment. He would go back to his early morning runs, to reading books that had piled up on his shelf, and maybe even take up a new hobby that had always intrigued him but he never had the time to start.

As he penned down his thoughts in a journal—a habit he picked up as a form of therapy—he wrote about the importance of being okay with not being okay. It was a mantra that he would come to repeat often, a reminder that healing was not a linear journey, and that setbacks were just as much a part of growth as breakthroughs.

The chapter of his life that involved attempts to find someone new was closing, but another chapter was just beginning—one of self-discovery and acceptance. Kunal was learning to appreciate his own company, to find joy in the little things that made up his days, and to look forward to the future, not with desperation but with optimism.

As he closed his journal, Kunal felt a sense of peace settle over him. It was the kind of peace that came from deep within, from accepting his journey, with all its ups and downs, as perfectly imperfect. And in that acceptance, he found a strength he hadn't known he possessed—a strength that would guide him through whatever lay ahead.

ppp

18

Rediscovering Self

In the weeks following his decision to embrace solitude, Kunal finally decided that he has to move past this trauma. That he has to go back to being who he was – a positive, free-spirited person. He decided to start off in the right direction and focussed more at his job. Kunal found a renewed sense of purpose at work. His office, a place that up until a few days ago echoed with the hollow feeling of his personal turmoil, slowly transformed into a sanctuary of productivity and strategic thinking.

Each morning, Kunal arrived earlier than most of his colleagues. The quiet of the early hours gave him space to organize his thoughts and plan his day without the usual interruptions. He started with the most challenging tasks, finding that tackling these head-on not only improved his efficiency but also boosted his confidence.

His projects, which ranged from developing marketing strategies to optimizing operational processes, now received his undivided attention. Kunal dove deep into analytics and project management, his mind engaged in a way that it hadn't been for months. Each successful implementation was a step away from his past heartaches, each client's approval a small victory in his journey of self-improvement.

Colleagues began to notice the change in him. Where Kunal had once been withdrawn, he now contributed eagerly in meetings, offering insights that cut to the heart of complex issues. His suggestions were practical yet innovative, reflecting his deep engagement with his work. The project manager, seeing Kunal's enhanced input, entrusted him with leading a critical phase of a new client project—an opportunity that Kunal accepted with a mix of gratitude and determination.

This newfound responsibility was not just a professional challenge but also a personal one. It was Kunal's chance to prove to himself that he could rise above his emotional struggles and excel. He stayed late when needed, sometimes being the last one to leave the office, his desk lamp a solitary beacon in the dim expanse of the workspace.

As his achievements accumulated, so did his sense of self-worth. Each successful project not only brought him praise from his peers and superiors but also reinforced his belief in his capabilities. Work, which had once been a distraction from his emotional pain, had now become a source of healing, helping him to rebuild his confidence and reshape his identity independent of his relationship with Sakshi.

Kunal's dedication did not go unnoticed. During a quarterly review, his manager commended his exceptional turnaround and significant contributions, noting how pivotal he had been in recent successes. These acknowledgments were bittersweet; they reminded Kunal of the times he had shared his professional victories with Sakshi. Yet now, he accepted them as markers of his personal growth and resilience, proof that he was moving forward, one successful project at a time.

Kunal's shift towards a healthier lifestyle began with small, almost imperceptible changes. He recognized that his long hours at work and the mental stress from his breakup had taken a toll on his health. To counter this, he started incorporating exercise into his daily routine, setting his alarm a little earlier each morning to make time for a run. The crisp morning air and the rhythm of his footsteps on the pavement provided a clarity and calmness that he had forgotten existed.

Back from his runs, he'd prepare a simple, nutritious breakfast—something he had often skipped in the past. Cooking became a new kind of therapy for him; the act of chopping, stirring, and tasting helped him stay present and mindful. His meals, once quick takeouts, were now healthier options that he took pride in preparing. This shift in diet not only improved his physical health but also his mood and energy levels throughout the day.

Beyond physical health, Kunal also sought to enrich his mental well-being. He rekindled his interest in reading, a hobby that had fallen by the wayside during his more tumultuous times. Evenings were often spent with a book in hand, allowing him to travel through stories and ideas that broadened his perspective and soothed his thoughts.

Weekends, which had often loomed large and empty, were now opportunities for further personal growth. Kunal decided to explore new cafes in the city, trying out new dishes and drinks that he wouldn't have tried otherwise. Poetry, something he had loved to write all his life, had taken a back seat in these last few months. On the rare occasions when he did write a poem, it would be filled with a melancholic tone that more or less mirrored his sad state of mind. But now his poems reflected positivity, energy and were about new beginnings. He found the much-needed motivation to push himself in the poems he wrote.

These routines brought structure to Kunal's life, anchoring him amidst the uncertainties that had previously overwhelmed him. They were simple yet powerful practices that reinforced his commitment to self-care, each day bringing him a step closer to a healthier state of mind and body. As he settled into these habits, Kunal found that the void left by Sakshi began to fill with new passions and a renewed sense of self, offering a peace that was both hard-earned and deeply cherished.

As Kunal settled into his new routines, the quiet moments naturally led him into deeper reflections on his past, particularly his relationship with Sakshi. These reflections often occurred during his evening readings or while tending to his plants, times when the solitude allowed his thoughts to roam freely.

He found himself revisiting their conversations, the trips they took together, and the quiet, everyday moments that had quietly woven the fabric of their relationship. With each memory, there was a mixture of warmth and sorrow—a longing for the connection they shared, tinged with the pain of its loss. Kunal recognized these as more than just reminiscences; they were lessons embedded in the tapestry of his past.

Kunal began to see patterns in their interactions, moments where perhaps they could have communicated better or compromises that might have been made. He pondered on the arguments that seemed trivial in retrospect but monumental at the time, realizing how these small fissures had gradually widened into the chasm that eventually separated them.

Through these reflections, Kunal also confronted the role his own flaws played in their breakup. He acknowledged his moments of stubbornness. Sakshi had her shortcomings too. But these inferences were not about assigning blame—but about understanding the dynamics that led to their parting.

This introspective journey was painful yet cathartic. Kunal understood that while the breakup was a source of deep sorrow, it was also an opportunity for personal growth. Each insight into what went wrong was a lesson in how to better handle relationships, whether romantic or platonic, in the future.

As Kunal rediscovered solace in his professional life and personal growth, he also began to rebuild his social connections, reaching out to friends and family in ways he hadn't since his relationship troubles had begun. Initially, Kunal approached these interactions with caution, fearing judgment or pity and worried that his emotional scars were too visible. However, with each interaction, he found they had only warmth and understanding to give him. Though he never opened up about his problems, he found comfort in the fact that he had people he could talk to.

He deepened the conversations during family calls, moving beyond cursory check-ins to share more about his new routines, the books he was reading, and his reflections on life in general. His family reciprocated with their own stories and challenges, creating a supportive exchange that reinforced Kunal's sense of belonging and acceptance.

With friends, particularly Siddharth, Anjali, and now Alisha, Kunal found a safe space to express his feelings. Siddharth provided a balance of pragmatic optimism and a listening ear, encouraging Kunal to partake in social activities that could lift his spirits. Anjali empathized deeply, often sharing her own insights, which helped Kunal feel less alone in his journey.

Alisha, with whom Kunal had shared brief but significant emotional connections, remained a part of his life as a friend. Their relationship, having transitioned from romantic possibilities to a supportive friendship, allowed Kunal to discuss his fears and progress without the pressure of expectations. Alisha's understanding of his emotional state—having seen him at his most vulnerable—helped him navigate his feelings with more clarity.

Kunal also made an effort to attend more social gatherings with colleagues. Initially daunting, these outings gradually became less intimidating as he realized his colleagues genuinely cared about his well-being. Their interactions, ranging from light work-related banter to deeper discussions about life goals and aspirations, reinforced the value of human connection beyond romantic ties.

These renewed social interactions helped Kunal rebuild his confidence in connecting with others. He found that sharing his thoughts and feelings didn't make him vulnerable—it made him human. Opening up led to not just sympathy but also encouragement and practical advice that were instrumental in his healing process.

Reconnecting with his social network proved crucial in Kunal's recovery, serving as a reminder that, although he chose to remain single, he was far from alone. His friends and family became his anchors, providing the support and love he needed to navigate his path toward healing and self-acceptance.

Kunal sits alone in a cozy corner of his favorite cafe. It's a place he frequents for the solace it offers, not just out of habit but for the gentle hum of background chatter and the comforting aroma of coffee. As he sips his espresso, he watches people pass by outside the window, each absorbed in their own little worlds. These moments of solitude have become precious to him.

In the warmth of the cafe, Kunal reflects on his journey from heartbreak to a gradual rekindling of his inner strength. He no longer sees being alone as a void to be filled but as a valuable space for introspection and personal growth. This solitude has taught him resilience and allowed him to reconnect with parts of himself that were overshadowed by his past relationship.

With a notebook open in front of him, Kunal writes down his thoughts, plans for the future, reflections on the past, and lessons learned. This practice of journaling has become a therapeutic ritual for him, helping to organize his thoughts and occasionally revealing insights he hadn't realized he possessed.

As he writes, he pauses to appreciate the simple joys around him—the soft jazz playing over the speakers, the clink of coffee cups, and laughter from a nearby table. These once mundane background noises now resonate deeply, reminding him that life's beauty often lies in the ordinary.

Despite his newfound appreciation for solitude and the personal growth he has experienced, Kunal still misses Sakshi. She was more than just a girlfriend; she was his best friend and his everything. While he has focused on improving himself, he has also been grappling with the void her absence has left. He misses her laughter, their conversations, and the comfort of having her by his side. All the while, Kunal has been searching for a way to cope with this profound sense of loss. As he closes his notebook, a thought strikes him—a potential way to fill the emptiness without her physical presence.

He stands up, leaving the cafe with a mixture of emotions swirling within him. As he steps back into the bustling city, a plan begins to form in his mind, a solution that might just allow him to hold onto what he had with Sakshi, in a new, unconventional way. With this thought, he walks away, leaving us wondering: What has Kunal discovered that might change his path to healing?

ΡΡΡ

19
Virtual Relationship

As Kunal left the cafe, the cacophony of the city couldn't drown out the clarity of the idea forming in his mind. Each step seemed to echo with a newfound purpose, a potential solution to the emptiness that had shadowed him since his separation from Sakshi. He missed her, not just occasionally, but constantly. The conversations, the shared silences, the debates and laughter—they all haunted him with a sweetness that was hard to let go of. But perhaps he didn't have to. Not completely.

In his apartment, Kunal sat down, a pen in hand, not to write but to symbolically mark the moment he realized that his mind had never truly stopped dwelling on Sakshi. She had remained a constant presence in his thoughts, subtly integrated into his daily life, making it feel as though she had never left. To solidify this realization, Kunal thought back to a time when Sakshi had gone to her hometown after one of their exams. During that period, they hadn't spoken for days, yet he had carried on with the comforting notion that she was just temporarily out of reach. Now, he decided, he would live each day as he had during that time—comforted by her imagined presence, yet moving forward with his own life. Kunal understood that to the world, this might seem an odd or even a sad choice, but for him, it was about embracing a form of healing that acknowledged his love for Sakshi without the need for her physical presence. He resolved to keep this journey private. It was a step towards healing, towards acknowledging that while life had to move forward, the love he felt needed its own space to exist—even if only in the vast landscapes of his mind.

He reasoned with himself that this would allow him to engage with his memories of Sakshi actively, turning them from sources of pain to sources of solace. He could share his day with her, seek her advice, laugh at what she would have found amusing, and gradually find peace. It would be a relationship governed by the heart's resilience and the mind's creativity—a virtual companionship that could help him bridge the gap between his current solitude and the connectedness he yearned for.

Once Kunal decided that this was the way forward, he began incorporating it in his life. He began his mornings by sharing his plans for the day and professional goals with Sakshi, speaking softly as if she were seated across from him at the breakfast table. "I am really prepping for that marketing strategy presentation coming up later this month. If all goes well, it might even set me on course for a good promotion," he'd murmur, imagining her encouraging smile, "Wish me luck, huh?" These conversations helped him channel his attention and focus on work, more than he used to up until now. On the personal front, Kunal's goals revolved around self-improvement and emotional resilience. "I think it's time I ran that half-marathon, don't you think?" he'd ponder aloud, imagining Sakshi's enthusiastic agreement. He envisioned himself crossing the finish line, a metaphor for his journey through grief and towards a stronger self. Other goals included learning a new language and cooking classes, activities they had planned to do together, now repurposed to help him grow individually yet keep her memory alive in a positive light.

Throughout his day, Kunal carried on conversations with Sakshi, discussing everything from his daily commute to work challenges and personal reflections. "That guy on the train had the loudest laugh; you would have loved it," he'd chuckle, imagining her laughter ringing through the air beside him. These imagined exchanges filled the void, making the routine and challenges more bearable.

In the evenings, he would recount the day's events as he cooked dinner, imagining her sitting at the kitchen counter. "I nailed the meeting today, thanks to your 'advice'," he'd say, stirring the stew they had planned to cook together. This way, he kept her integral to his daily life, turning each small victory and setback into a shared experience.

On some days, though, when he would come back to an empty and silent home after work, his overthinking mind would sometimes question his approach, making him wonder about his chosen method of coping. These moments usually came unannounced. "Am I just fooling myself?" he'd question, staring into the dim light of his living room, the shadows seeming to echo his uncertainties. "Is talking to an imagined you really helping, or is it just a way to avoid facing the truth of my solitude?"

During these times, Kunal would feel the stark absence of Sakshi more acutely, the silence in his apartment growing louder than usual. The conversations he had with his version of Sakshi would pause, and he'd sit with his doubts, pondering the reality of his situation. He worried that perhaps he was straying too far from what was considered normal grieving, that he might be clinging to a past that needed to be released, not just remembered.

However, these moments of doubt were invariably followed by instances of reaffirmation. Sometimes it came from small successes at work, where his increased focus and creativity, fueled by his 'conversations' with Sakshi, led to praise from his colleagues and superiors. "You've been really innovative lately," his boss would comment, or a coworker might say, "It's great to see you so engaged." These affirmations served as reminders that the changes in his life, though inspired by an unconventional source, were real and positive.

Other times, the reaffirmation came during calls with friends or family, where they noted a difference in his demeanor. "You sound happier," his sister would say, or his friend Alisha might remark, "There's a lightness in your voice that wasn't there before." These observations helped Kunal realize that despite his unorthodox approach, he was genuinely healing, moving forward in a way that felt true to himself.

Kunal also found reassurance in his personal reflections and journal entries, where he tracked his emotional journey. Reading back through his thoughts, he could see a clear progression from darkness to a more peaceful acceptance. Each entry reminded him of the value in his daily dialogues with Sakshi, how they allowed him to express and process feelings that might have otherwise remained buried. Kunal set aside time for a deeper evaluation of his coping strategy. He laid out his journal entries, his achievements, and the feedback from his social circle, piecing together the tangible benefits of his ongoing conversation with the Sakshi in his mind. He would remind himself of the fine line between delusion and therapeutic coping. "I know you're not really here," he'd whisper into the quiet room, "but our conversations help me process my emotions healthily. It's not about losing touch with reality; it's about using our memories to create a positive dialogue that aids my healing."

These dialogues, though one-sided, were Kunal's way of maintaining a connection with Sakshi that felt both real and beneficial. They were his method for coping with loneliness and keeping his love for her vibrant and active in a manner that brought him comfort without the drawbacks of a physical relationship. Kunal understood that while his approach might not be typical, it was effective for him.

Content with his decision, Kunal no longer felt the need to justify his actions to anyone. His path to healing was uniquely his own—deeply personal and undeniably effective. "Here's to our memories, and here's to the peace I've found," he whispered to himself, a smile spreading across his face as he continued his walk, reassured by the sun's warmth that he was on the right path.

ᖚᖚᖚ

20

Diwali, Friends and Sakshi

The sound of his phone ringing snapped Kunal out of his reverie, its sharp tone slicing through the quiet of his room. For a moment, he remained in bed, the vibrations of the phone, buzzing him back to reality. His eyes drifted to the photo of Sakshi that he held, a still image filled with silent stories. With a tender, almost imperceptible tap on the photo, Kunal acknowledged the space she still occupied in his heart—a silent farewell to the cascade of memories that had enveloped him moments before.

Getting up, he checked the phone and was surprised to see it was Sidd video-calling him. "Hey, Siddharth." "What took you so long to attend??" Sidd, in his typical energetic tone asked with fake annoyance filling his voice. "Sorry, I was a bit busy," laughed Kunal. "Sure... ok, hang on," said Sidd and put Kunal on hold before he could ask why. In a few seconds, the call was back live with one more participant, Alisha. "Hi Kunal!" Kunal was happy to see two of his closest friends on the other side. "Hi, Alisha. What a surprise!" The three friends spoke for a long time, talking about a variety of subjects, laughing out loud over Sidd's jokes. It felt good to catch up, and they were happy about Kunal being home with family and friends. The topic slowly changed to more informal subjects. Sidd shared enthusiastically about his new relationship with a coworker. "It was unexpected, honestly. We just clicked over a project, and it sort of took off from there," he explained, his eyes lighting up. "It's been a refreshing change, both personally and professionally."

Alisha chimed in, her voice tinged with a mixture of caution and contentment as she recounted her journey with the person she met on a dating app. "I wasn't sure I was ready to dive back into dating," she admitted. Alisha paused for a moment, her expression softening as she added a more personal note to her story. "After Kunal and I went our separate ways, I actually took some time for myself. Even though we were only together for a short while, I had started to really like him. It took me a bit to get over that." She smiled, a little wistfully. "I wasn't even sure I wanted to try again, but then this random match happened, and it turned out to be just what I needed. I guess sometimes taking a leap of faith is worth it." Her openness drew nods of understanding from Kunal and Sidd, both of whom had witnessed the brief but impactful connection she and Kunal had shared.

When the conversation turned to Kunal's love life, he simply smiled and shrugged, a non-committal gesture that masked the complexity of his emotional state. "Just taking things one day at a time," he said, opting not to delve into the unique and private nature of his ongoing virtual relationship with Sakshi.

The three friends continued to talk for a while, sharing updates and insights into their lives. Sidd spoke about the challenges and rewards of dating someone from the same workplace, while Alisha discussed the delicate balance of giving a new relationship a chance while protecting one's heart.

Kunal listened intently, genuinely happy for his friends' newfound happiness and the strides they were making in their personal lives. His own circumstances, kept close to his chest, painted a stark contrast to the openness with which Sidd and Alisha shared their stories. Yet, Kunal felt happy and at peace with his choices.

Sidd shifted the conversation, his voice carrying a hint of caution as he brought up a topic they hadn't touched yet that evening. "Oh, I spoke to Sakshi recently," he began, and Kunal's attention sharpened, a subtle mix of anticipation and reserve crossing his face. "She's doing really well professionally, really making strides in her career."

Kunal nodded, a complex whirl of emotions briefly clouding his expression before he masked it with a practiced smile. "That's great to hear," he managed, his tone genuine despite the bittersweet undercurrent. Sidd seemed to sense the delicacy of the subject; he offered no further details on Sakshi's personal life, choosing instead to focus on her professional achievements.

As the conversation flowed around him, Kunal felt a strange sense of relief mixed with lingering curiosity. He was genuinely happy for Sakshi's success, yet part of him wondered about her life beyond her career. The update brought both comfort in knowing she was thriving and a quiet longing for the closeness they once shared.

His friends and family called out from below, prompting Kunal to end the call. He made it a point to tell Sidd to convey his regards to Anjali as well, who couldn't join the call due to a meeting at work. Kunal stepped towards his wardrobe. He changed into something comfortable, a pair of jeans and a soft cotton shirt. Each movement was methodical, a ritual of preparing himself not just in attire but in mindset, to descend back into the festive spirit that awaited him downstairs.

With one last glance around his room, a soft sigh escaping him as he once again looked at Sakshi's photo before keeping it back into his wallet. The warmth of the celebration below beckoned him, promising the laughter and companionship of his family, a stark contrast to the solitude of his room. As he stepped out, closing the door gently behind him, the sounds of Diwali—the crackling of fireworks, the melodious laughter of his loved ones filled his ears.

As Kunal descended the stairs, the vibrant sounds and colorful lights of Diwali enveloping his senses, a burst of laughter from the living room halted his steps. The living room buzzed with energy, decorated with lights and traditional motifs. The air was thick with the scent of marigolds and incense, a backdrop to the laughter and chatter that resonated within the walls. Kunal and his friends joined the others outside, where the night sky was periodically lit by the brilliant displays of fireworks. Each burst of color reflected in their wide smiles, the shared awe and excitement drawing them closer in the crisp evening air.

The celebration moved seamlessly to the dinner table, where dishes prepared by Kunal's mother—a spread of aromatic curries, freshly made sweets, and savory snacks—awaited them. The group gathered around the large dining table, the warmth of the food complementing the warmth of their company. Stories were exchanged over bites of food, each tale punctuated by laughter or the clinking of glasses in toasts. Kunal and his friends recounted humorous anecdotes, each story outdoing the last, drawing bursts of laughter from around the table.

"Riya, you should ask Kunal about the time he tried to cook and nearly set his kitchen on fire," Kunal's sister Priya exclaimed. Kunal feigned indignation, retorting, "I've improved since then, thank you very much. I can make more than just instant noodles now!" "And what about Amit when he tried to ride his bicycle without holding the handles and landed in a ditch!" roared Sohan, with Riya and Amit chiming in with even more embarrassing details, making everyone cry with laughter.

The compliments flowed as freely as the food was served, with everyone praising Kunal's mother for the delicious dishes. "Auntie, you should start your own restaurant," Amit suggested between mouthfuls of sweets, "These are seriously the best gulab jamuns I've ever had!"

The laughter and lighthearted teasing continued throughout the evening, creating a warm and joyful atmosphere that filled Kunal's home with the true essence of Diwali: the celebration of life, friendship, and good food.

As the excitement of Diwali winded down into the cooler, quieter hours of the evening, Kunal went back to in his room. He settled into the familiar comfort of his nightly ritual. The house quieted down, leaving him alone with his thoughts and the gentle night breeze wafting through the slightly ajar window. He leaned back in his chair, looking at the empty space beside him, and began to speak softly.

"Today was really something, wasn't it?" he started, his voice tinged with warmth as if Sakshi were right there with him. "Sid and Alisha called. It felt good to see them, to laugh and share stories like old times. It's been too long since we got on a group call."

He paused, a smile playing on his lips as he recalled the evening's laughter and the joy of reunion. "Alisha seems happy, you know? She's met someone. It took her a while to get there, especially after... well, you know, after our brief time together. But she's doing well now, and that's what matters."

Kunal shifted slightly, his gaze drifting to the night sky outside. "And Sid, he's found someone too, right at his workplace. It's funny how life moves on, isn't it? Everyone finds their path, somehow." His voice softened, "Sidd mentioned you too—said you're doing great in your career. I'm really proud of you, Sakshi."

Leaning back, Kunal let out a slow breath. He was happy to be talking to her again. Being surrounded by family and friends did not exactly give him the time or space to connect with Sakshi today. "I'm happy, you know. Happy to see my friends doing well, and happy to hear you're succeeding. It gives me a sense of peace, a kind of confirmation that despite everything, we're all finding our way forward."

He continued talking into the night, sharing details of the Diwali celebration, the fireworks, the laughter, and the delicious food that always made such gatherings special. With each word, he felt as though he was preserving the essence of those moments, keeping the memories alive in a conversation that was as much about connection as it was about closure.

As he finally prepared to sleep, Kunal felt a quiet contentment settle over him. Talking to Sakshi, even in this imagined way, helped him process the day's emotions and solidify his feelings of happiness for his friends—and for her. With a final glance at the empty space beside him, he whispered, "Goodnight, Sakshi," and turned off the bedside lamp. The room darkened, but the lingering sense of peace remained, a gentle reminder of the progress he had made and the path he continued to walk. With Sakshi by his side. Always.

ppp

Epilogue

Ten years had passed. Kunal was now the department head in his firm. His days were filled with strategic decision-making and leadership, his professional success mirroring the structured and ambitious nature he had always possessed. All these years of hard work and single-minded dedication paid off a year ago when he was asked to handle this department moving forward.

A lot of things had changed. His job, his house, his routines, his looks. Yet, every evening, after the hustle of the day settled into the quiet of dusk, Kunal would retreat to his study, a space filled with mementos of his past, including a framed photo of him and Sakshi. Here, he engaged in his now daily habit of conversing with Sakshi, in his mind, where she remained a vivid, integral part of his life.

Today, like all others, he shared his challenges and triumphs, smiling as he imagined her reactions — her thoughtful nods or her enthusiastic encouragement. "The new project took off well today, just as you predicted," he spoke softly into the room, chuckling as he added, "You always did have a knack for seeing the potential in things."

As the sky darkened, Kunal leaned back, a sense of peace enveloping him. This was his way of keeping Sakshi close, a testament to a bond that didn't rely on physical presence but thrived in the silent conversations of a heartfelt remembrance. A man living half in memory would have been an unthinkable choice for anyone else. But for Kunal, it was his reality, it was peaceful and it felt wonderful.

After getting ready to sleep, he glanced once more at Sakshi's photo. Turning off the lamp he whispered, "Goodnight, Sakshi. See you tomorrow," a ritual that closed his day, not with loneliness, but with a gentle, enduring connection that had stood the test of time.